T0147760

RECIPROCITY

RECIPROCITY

Lark Voorhies

iUniverse, Inc.
New York   Bloomington

Reciprocity

Copyright © 2010 by Lark Voorhies

All rights reserved. No part of this book may be used or reproduced by any means, graphic, electronic, or mechanical, including photocopying, recording, taping or by any information storage retrieval system without the written permission of the publisher except in the case of brief quotations embodied in critical articles and reviews.

This is a work of fiction. All of the characters, names, incidents, organizations, and dialogue in this novel are either the products of the author's imagination or are used fictitiously.

iUniverse books may be ordered through booksellers or by contacting:

iUniverse
1663 Liberty Drive
Bloomington, IN 47403
www.iuniverse.com
1-800-Authors (1-800-288-4677)

Because of the dynamic nature of the Internet, any Web addresses or links contained in this book may have changed since publication and may no longer be valid. The views expressed in this work are solely those of the author and do not necessarily reflect the views of the publisher, and the publisher hereby disclaims any responsibility for them.

ISBN: 978-1-4502-0066-0 (sc)
ISBN: 978-1-4502-0068-4 (dj)
ISBN: 978-1-4502-0067-7 (ebk)

Printed in the United States of America

iUniverse rev. date: 12/23/2009

Prelude to a Fit

Start in, black. Fade in sexy, jazz music. We set the scene, as we cross the New York City Sky Line. Scanning across the skyline, we rest on the Manhattan Residence of Marcus Erickson. We hear, the sounds of passion. Fade out sexy music. Fade into: Two people, mid-coitle. Cheri Coles, and, Marcus. Going through the motions, something, doesn't seem, "connected." Marcus, begins to moan.

"You gonna go with me?" "No, sweetheart, wait." "You gonna go with me?" "A minute, please, hold on." "You gonna go, Cheri?" "Yes, wait "Come on." "Marcus..." 'You gonna go? Come on, Cheri, you want this?" Panicking, "wait!" "Ahhhh...J" Too late. Zero, and, blast off. A, "No... !" echoes, into, the, night, sky.

Pleasure seizure has begun. Well, for Marcus, anyway. Cheri, noticeably frustrated, turns over onto her side. A moment, and, she turns back over, in the attempt to initiate dialogue, only to fmd Marcus, dead to the world. Pure exasperation, as she "hanumphs" back over onto her side. Staring off blankly, into the night's stars, she's heard, so often about, At the love amiss. That she missed.

She takes opportunity to think back, to a time where it was, oh, so different.

The light was so bright that, early, morning. She could feel it, filter, across her baby-soft skin. Nights before, had been, incredible, in the category of whirlwind evenings. Dined at New York's fmest. Lifted by 'copter ride, to explore the glorious sky. Romanced, on the Farmer's Bridge, near Tavern on the Green. She could field the way to layers, extreme. It was a sweeping celebration of five, wonderful years. To which, she remained, loyal, to her first, true, love. It was that night, that he proposed. That night, that he pledged his unequivocal love. It was that night, that she, unequivocally, surrendered, to allow him her first.

It was incredible. First touch. First kiss. From, the Genesis of it, through, to the, amazing, revelation. Old wives tales had nothing on this. I-fe was so tender. So kind. His, every, word, properly placed, precious, gems. Each, an, invitation, into this new world of ecstatic, bliss.

She, remembers, sensing, fields, and, amber waves of grain. Purple mountain majesties, covered her sight. She, could hear the ring of history, merging, with the song of the present. Passion had a name, and, it was M-A R-C-U-S! She cheered for him from within the very depths of her soul. Disneyland, and , time machines filled her head. Pleasure was as new, and, as free for the taking, as countryside wildflowers. Young love, perfumed the air. "Days like this" by Jessie Belvin Played in her heart, and in her minds eye, she could see him. Handsome. Powerful. Full of steam. His hands, his lips, his thighs, all drove her to a peak she could hardly come down from. Her hands, scaled his eyes, and, his back. Through, to, the top of his thought. She panted, smiled, and, wailed. Until, theft breath met And, then, and then, and then, they pushed play all over again.

This time, river beds lapped at her for sensation. Waves took her by current. Depths of desire, pulled her further into his, amorous, delight. Meaningfully, sensually, he played with her every intention. Danced, within her wildest dreams. Mastered, her amore. His, "summer breeze", sang, sweetly, to, virgin, ear. Which, had, never, heard such, irresistible, utterance, and, delivery. Height, was coming. Height, was coming. Height, was coming. And then, finally, she, realized, who, "God" meant.

These days, they didn't "talk" much. Halls, echo, with, love gone past. Hands touch, with a loathsome sensation. For, she hates to offer of her essential charms to a man who, insists, upon, auto-piloting, his. His hands. no longer spoke, they complained. Her body, no longer knew what he wanted. She profaned. Protest, now, there dance.

These days, they neither, knew where they began, nor, where they would finish. Where, the, tide would gather, nor, where, the, mute, went, endless. Where, kisses used to blow her away, they, now, just blew into the wind. "Away, away," she called. "Come here, come here," he insisted. Their language, all, but, at babble of confuse.

A touch, that used to be electric, was, now, an, awkward, pause. An, emergence, of signal, to change the subject, by way of immediate position. Glances, used to tell all, to a tempo sublime. Now, they, merely, peeked, and, remised. Devastated and unsure. Instead of beaming, from that peak of ecstatic bliss, she, now, exploded with frustration. Screaming, from the core of her being,

"I need off this ride! I need off this ride! I need off this ride!"

Chapter Out!

Here, stands the, modest, residence of Mona Strathern. Cheri's Mother. An area of life, where newly weds have become families, and executives get their full motivation to conquer the professional world. As, the, "homes", far outnumber the houses, within this quaint, little, world of hope and glory. From a cozy little window, we hear a piano playing.

Enter Mona's living room, as the music plays on. We take in the electric, warm, surroundings that make this house a home. Leafs of heritage,. sprinkle, in clusters of photograph, and, various spoils of travel. Giving the indication of a home, filled, with love and wisdom. Looking in closely, we see that it is Cheri that plays so, beautifully, on the, family, piano. Vivaldi, plays, delightfully, through her, Mozart, trained fmgers. She closes eye, to feel the intimacy of the keys and tones, that bring the notes to glorious life.

Her sister, Dana, sits, contemplatively, in the corner, reading. Still, in the executive attire that gives away her day job. She allows the music to tone her into her other world of dance. "Only the classics! Only the classics!" Her mother would insist.

As a child, Dana was the star of the family. Why, with ballet, jazz, and, tap, vocal lessons, and, drama class, she charmed her way to elite, favored position. That life lasted well in to her young adulthood. Now, it was going to take an act of God to keep her within her daddy's Granny smith. "I don't want to be your daddy anymore." He told her with a certain directness one day. "I want, now, to be your father." Talk about a heart attack! That life-giving vessel did not beat the length of her secret. She couldn't live without being her father's favorite. She swallowed heavily, and, running cold with pause, her sight began to pale. Only a prayer could save her now, as, this transition was so, new, to her. She could sense the difference between daddy and father were worlds apart. Would he really leave her behind as he had insinuated? Or, was this some, notional, clue, some reverse coach, designed to throw her for a loop, as he done so many times before. Why, he would toss and twirl his shooting star like a baton. She had always led the parade. Why so drastic a shift, in their o-so-perfect relationship, now? Was he ready to move on with some major life change that she, in her ripe persona, hadn't laid out, appropriate, attention to? Had he been too indulgent with her? Was he now ready to induct Cheri in her stead? "I mean, sure she aces math, and, the sciences with an ease that does touch his heart, and she's brilliant with the classics, And, when she plays, he does go to some far away place that she can't quite reach. But she's never been able to call to his soul the way my performances do. And, her formulaic breakthroughs have never brought him to tear's, as do my song. I suppose, both she, and, I had gotten used to his nodding approval at her achievements, and his breathless "thank you's" with mine. Well, I'm not ready to give that up, yet." She thought. "Why, I was set to dance this path, all of my life." Gathering her overgrown sense of herself, for she had turned a wonderful, sapphire tone. She, collected the words, "Yes, father. Of course, father. Indeed, father." Having received his smile, she turned inward to treasure, and, build strategy, for his further approval.

"Cheri, Dana!" Mona calls out to them, as the music stops. "Yes, mom!" Cheri responds. "You two, will be joining me in here while I do this, or, am I going to finish this on my own, again?" She, sings out with a tint of command. "Why does she get a 'mom?" Dana, cried out under rumpled breath. "We, must not be as close as I once believed." She, thought. Then, she began to, reflect, on all of their, heart-to-heart, "talks," as, she liked to put it. Cheri, coined them "discussions." She, was always so mature, always the voice of reason, and, always ,first ,choice, whenever mother, or, father were beyond reach, or, were too upset with her to listen. And, she, did love to talk. Cheri, on the other hand, hadn't a need for such, as, she, always had the piano, with which to express, and, order her, deepest, intention. Dana, grew heated with a, new, panic. "How did I not see these things? I've always been the intuitive one. Why, Cheri has always had the world that she goes off into. And, I, have always had center stage." The, heat grew downright solar. "I'm not going to take this sifting down! That's, for sure!" She perceived, her eyes, now pulsing with a, darkness, that did distort her sight. "I must do something. Immediately!" She, insisted. "Mom. Well, mother," she, clears her throat, "we're, on the way!"

Mona, who has never been, shy, with her girls, and, who has, always, called to attention with immediate results, gives her preparations the once-over, to, secure, that her, arrangements, have been ordered, well. The, confirmation, checks, and, so, she receives her two sparkling gems, with the love and ardor of a fried, and, true matron, of the fold. Her, glow, the result of years of joy, and, respect. Handmade. Her, lovely, smile, and, commanding eyes, tell, tale traits of having survived, and, been, refined, by the demanding changes, coming, of this $_{20}$th Century.

As, the girls arrive to the kitchen by their, very, individual, ways, Dana, naturally, arrives ahead of Cheri, and, is, first, to witness the dynamic spread, as usual ,is well thought out, and, in its various stages of completion. Cheri, well at home, breezes by Dana, who, remembers her, Akili, and, coasts on her trepidation. "Well, don't just stand there, peering at it like that, Dana. It's not going to bite you." She, necessitates. "Cheri," she instructs, "this way. I'll need you, here."

Leading her daughter around to her, pre-designed, station, she, lovingly, lays out the law, of the task, that Cheri will perform. Dana, who looks on, with an increasing helplessness, interrupts. "I, don't think anyone else will be doing that, either, if, I have anything to do with it. Bit; that is." She, torts. She, succeeds, in having them share a laugh, but, as Mona's attention returns to Cheri, she finds that she can't resist. "Really, mom. It's, far, beyond, the, natural, time, for me to know this." She states. "I'm, so, unnaturally, behind .."" "Well, Cheri, will be married soon." She glows. "I, can retire, and, she can show you ." She resolutes, knowing Dana's motive, as, her mind goes to. "Married. That's something, I, remember, all too well." She, reflects. "And, to think, some of my best years are, here. Catching, up, with me." She, ponders this a moment. Then, calls to mind, her, wedding, day.

It, was the very, age, of, pastel, vibrancy. Captain & Teoneele, were #1 hits, And, earth Wind & Fire, the blast. The, air was, sweet. And, love was, forever. Everything, seemed to have the touch of, sunshine. Including his smile. Robert Coles, the love of her life. 6'S", distinguished. Tall, dark, and, highly, intelligent. A, freedom, fighter, he, won, more cases, than, Martin, gave speeches. So, many, individual, rights, to fight for. So, many, lives, depended, upon, his, passion, for moral ethics. His, drive, to stand, in, the, heat, of, that, which is right. And, fight, he did. For, he, survived, discrimination, in all of its evil, and, wanted, nothing, more, than to share, in his, liberties.

It, was a, beautiful, wedding, and, a, lovely, marriage. First, the two of them, and, then, the four. Life, couldn't, be, more, sweet. Why, with his, budding career, and, her, book writes, they, toned, quite, well,, with the town, and, its, toasts. Family, life, was, her, greatest, memory. Keeping, up, with, social, etiquette, a game, at which, to, play, well. So, keeping up with the Jones's, was, never, quite, the, feat, it, proved, to be, for most. A, car, here, a, town home, there. They, swiftly, made ascent, up, the, ladder's, status, when, it was the time, to do so. Quite, naturally. Keeping, perfect, rhythm.

"I'll, only, show you. I'll, never, give, you ,any, of my, secret, you, hear?" Cheri snaps. Returning, them, all, to, the, plane, with, whence, they, had, all, realmed. "Where, is, this, coming from?" Mona, protests. "Why, so, harsh, with your, sister? Sounds, more, like, Marcus, talking, to me. Is, that, young man, still, trying, to, rewrite, my, little, girl, to fit into, his, life?"

Mona, remembers, all, too, well, the, women's, rights, movements, of her age. The, N.O.W., campaigns, that, shaped, her, entire, personal, scope. Not to mention, the, entire, vision, with, which, she, saw, herself, as, an, individual. Strong, will, sailed, her, right, through, any, ostracism, she, may, have, experienced, in her quest, for the achievement, of; feminine, accountability, and, independence. She, would, know, nothing, less, for her, daughters.

Cheri, knew, the, best, path, in this, conversation, was, not, that of, least, resistance. It, was, straight forward. Facing, head, on, the, issue, they, both, knew, to be, apparent. "That, may, be. However, I don't agree. I'm only being direct." She, defended. "Oh, this, is not, my, child." Rebutted, Mona. "Child?" She, pronounces. "Mother, in my opinion, its', obvious, that you, don't, know, me, either. Glad, to, know, that, after 8-years, we, can, fmally, agree, on, something." Cheri, declares. Mona, measures, Chcri. Cheri, covers. Mona, recalls, the, spicy, personality, of her, daughter. And, has, even, admired, its high points, as, the, fight, to, survive, familial, infamousy. She's, always, been, a, contender. In, life, she, was, first,. In, my love, she, was, prime. And, in, the, core, of; my, beats, she, is, my, all time, favorite. She's, everything, I'd, hope, to be, in her, young, lifetime. She's, met, and, exceeded, all, expectation. I'm, delighted, to be a, Mom. I've, been, guided, to the, special. And, now, I, shall, succeed, in, leading, the, outstanding. "I, know, just, what, to, say." She, clears, her, throat. "My dear, I'm going to pass on to you, what my mother told me. And, that, which, her mother, told her. 'If you're going to set yourself up to be anything in life, make it 'happy.'

The, advice, was so simple to follow, that it was, anti-climax, to its very, build. Cheri's, blank, expression, so indicative, of her, comprehensive, process ,made this, glaringly, obvious. They, all, take a, moment, to absorb. Dana, breaks the, silence. "How, did you, and, dad do it?" Indicating, her, naked, ring, finger. "Honey, we didn't" She, matter, of; facts. Returning, the, spin, of; events, to, the, accurate, present. "You, know, what I mean mother."

Dana, presses. "Before, the divorce, you, and, dad, I mean, father, were always, so, passionate. I, don't remember, ever, feeling, anything, but, extremes, of; happy, whenever, we were, all, together. And, now..." she, digresses, trailing, off; into, the, central, figure, of; her, contemplation. In, wonder, regarding, her, singular, concerns. "Well," her, mother, begins, "now, your, father, is a big-shot, muperhousen, and, a, few, other, unmentionables, that, I, won't, spoil your dinner with." She warned. "Mother," Dana, examines, at, length, "I'm, speaking, even, of; afterwards. The, respect, just, never, went away."

Mona, acknowledges, the, value, within, the, point, just made. She, decides, to speak, further. "With, your, father," she, begins, "and, I've, never, shared, this, with, you, girls, before. It, is my, belief; that, we were, very, fortunate. It, has, been, to, my, experience, that, life, speaks, very, clearly. And, if; you, listen, opportunity, is, never, far." The, two, soak this in. Faces, blank. Hearts, open. In, order, to, catch, the, full, meaning, Dana, must, intercept, once, more. "So, you're, saying...?" She, insinuates. Mona, fills, in. " What, I'm, saying, is, there, is, a, time, when, your, father, and, I, were, happiest, together. And, there, was, a, time, where, it was, evident, we, were, going, to be, happiest, apart. We, 'listened', that's, all." As, the, room, chews, on, that, food, for, thought. "Life, grants, you, permission, to, seize, the, opportunity." She, continues. "If; you, don't, take, **it,** it's, just, going, to, run, you, through."

Mona, reaches, over, to, touch, her, daughter's, hand. Intending, to, stress, the, underlying, point, she, had, been, so, vocal, about, on, so, many, prior, occasions. Now, she, really, wanted, to, attempt, markation, home, through, squinted, grip. "Make, it, happy, honey. Make, it, happy."

Cheri, ponders, the, levels, of her, mother's, fervor, and, devouted, statement. They'd, always, done, so, well, at, it. Was, this, a, warning? Concurring, present, moment, she, hadn't, realized, there, was, a, science, to, it. "Have. Have, nots." She, started, to, think. Concurring, this, moment, it. Had, not, occurred, to, her, there, was, a, formula. It, had, always, just, been, a, rhythm, she, followed. With, her, sheltered, world, shrinking, in, seizure, it, is, now, her, tempo, that, is, uneasy. Where, she, once, flowed, freely, she, would, now, have, to, work. Dana, studies, her, sister's, silence. Before, she, has, a, chance, to, panic, Mona, with, timely, preparedness, intercedes. "Well, with that said, let's get back to this lesson before Dana truly poisons someone of us." "With Cheri's attitude, it might not be the food that does it." Dana laughs, throwing a knowing look to Cheri, who gestures her comeback with, knife. "I don't exactly apologize, but I can't eat those things that you try to pass off as home cooked meals." Cheri offers. "I'll have to agree, Dana, you are my child in every way, with exception of; that. God only knows what happened there." Mona defends. The room quiets once again, as food, again, becomes the center of attention. They, silently, each cater their own task. The pace sails at a peaceful buzz. Each cadence a happy meditation. Then a thought sets in, Mona surfaces. "Imagine, that boy, trying to change my daughter! He's lightheaded, but, from that high horse he rides, that's no standing, at all. Who does he think he is, your father? Trust me, Cheri, a mother knows, the attitude is the first thing to go hard when your love life has gone soft. You should make new everyday what you have at the start. See it as fine cuisine, and, you should do quite well." She remarks. "Dana, baby, we are going to have a time with you."

New York State of Mnd

Cheri loved the open air, and, leapt at the opportunity to take it in wherever, and whenever possible. She'd always found herself embracing that gust of freedom gracing her presence at the open door. Though trained to trust the safety of familiar spaces, usually confined, it was the welcomed premiere of each, vast unknown that captured her innate sense of creative flow. To explore and conquer was her birthright, and, by nature she seemed to easily win the untamed world with an ease irresistible to the novice and the seasoned professional. Mind, body, spirit. Hook, line, and, sinker, living, was an ascent of sport.

Eager to catch life by the tail, while thriving at the head of it, taught to follow, she adventured the lead of her every free will, and, on the streets of New York, she was no precocious pansy. Poised. intact, she could keep rhythm with the meanest of city beats.

Cheri steps out from her mother's mystic brownstone onto the city streets, and, into life fresh with concern. Taking in the metropolitan air in deep gulfs, and, inspired satisfaction. Shrugging off her mother's predictable warning, and, her woeful reality, the evidence of forced confidence overrides her trepidation. This is evident in every step, as she prepares to accept the inevitable. Would she, and, Marcus make it, or, would they be better apart? She limps on upon this scale of tones, and, shapes that bum, and, cool equally, rounding the corner to the subway city entrance. She blends away from the more civil tempo of the suburban streets in order to carefully descend down into the active pulse of her subterranean metropolis. Finessing protocol, she arrives at the train stop. Each stage acclimating her to this all too familiar shift in sub culture. As soon as the "Y" train is announced over the automatic system, she herds her way into the subway car.

Getting seated, she settles, and, pops in the extensions to her I-Pod. Getting into her opus. In tune with this train vibe, she can be seen tapping her fingers, an, toes in time. Fluent with the frequency, she's timed her soul to the point of exit which is always announced. With the conformation of this, she gathers her belongings, herds out, and, prances to the arrangement of Manhattan City streets.

Changing soundtracks, Cheri takes on a whole new vantage point of the New York experience. New York, the city of revolution, and, world culture. New York, the city where the varied caricatures of life come to play. We take note of the various, subway characters. The on, and, off traffic. The in-between stops. Scoping in on city life, we take notice of the hot dog vendors, and, their multi-tasking businesses. Dog walkers, with many, excited, big dogs. Dog walkers with many, excited, little dogs. Owners with their tamed ones. We see the varied, staple, New York city street performers (the mimes, the sketch artists, vocalists, street dancers, etc.). The red, to yellow, to green city, traffic light instruction. The tail pipe exhaust. The many armies of vehicle break lights. Toll booth traffic, and, storm of change being deposited into the passing baskets. The joggers, the walkers, the bike riders. The active agenda of each, and, every individual. The ambitious spirit as far as you can see. All housed, and, expressed within the wealth of design, and, barrier throughout every living, breathing oraphis of this charcoaledstained, world renound watering hole. We fmd Cheri within this sea of malaise, well at ease, and, quite at home. Taking it all in through the order, and melody of the classics. New York; the world, and, its "Gritty Ballet."

We now discover Cheri having arrived to her point of destination. The establishment towers, and, is imposing to her delicate framing. Known by her. Unobstructed, and, quite unbound, she advances into the building.

Finally, arriving to Marcus' place of business, we catch up with Cheri breezing through the embrace of the front, revolving doors, pacing on through the atriumed lobby, ultimately landing herself into the upward bound elevator. The sundial-like floor indicator correctly confu-ms each, and, every floor, as the cabin ascends. As Cheri arrives, and, steps out of the elevator, and, into the entryway, her sonata comes to a lovely conclude. Removing her headphones, she welcomes in the world once again.

Placed in the entryway to the office of Mr. Marcus Erickson, Cheri braces herself for what she senses to be an entire obstacle of unpleasantries. Stepping up to the reception desk, she approaches with caution. Beginning to swallow, and, breath heavily. Feeling the coursing pulse of her heart, and, vein. "Hey Donna?" She reaches out for the attention of Donna Miles, Receptionist to Bernstein & Lindenplatt L.L.P. 'Tis late in the afternoon, and, Cheri knows the line up of events like the back of her hand, for it is as familiar to her as is, color by number. Today, however, this variation to the charge in the air has left her quite color blind. In flashes of mildly rising panic, she remembers her Father. His art lessons, how he taught her to flow with the brush, blend in with the texture. Today, she would canvas this.

This reflex of memory affords her a new confidence with which to rinse away the now fading hysteria with each passing increment of time. "Ms. Coles." Cheri responds immediately, delightfully being cut off from her attack of confidence. "One moment, and, I'll get Mr. Erickson for you ." She confirms, as Cheri satisfies one, last, and, complete exhalation. For her well-grounded grace has won the days point again, first round. "Thank you." Cheri returns, poising herself as Marcus is paged, and, and, she hears her usual, "Mr. Erickson, Ms. Coles is here. Certainly. Ms. Coles, you may go on through."

As, she levels the doors, and, scales on through these well built, yet humble halls of justice, Cheri styles herself the eye of the storm. Gaining power with each step. She prepares to appease the eye of her affection, her fiancé, and, soon to be husband. With fully trained composure, she arrives at the office of Mr. Marcus Erickson, and, greets him with an absolutely, electric smile.

Properly involved in a business call, he, on the usual, casually directs her to be seated. Simultaneous to her own instinct. Per her response, 'tis apparent that this aloof reserve has been a recent, and, even on-going event in the rift, and, growing differences between them. Making her way to a comfortable sit, she anticipates the wait to be a while. This being the usual routine, she arms herself in preparedness. Headphones in place, she plucks out a book, and, proceeds to make the most of her time in limbo. "Looks like it's going to be a bumpy ride." She hints to herself.

"Exactly." Marcus excites. "So, the 'what to do' is that we draw from the preliminary position of their argument, and, gamble against their weak point, attention to detail." He explains. "Listen, this whole thing will be concluded in a week's time. Believe me" He confirms. Marcus, two years strong with the firm, aims at becoming partner. To cliché, he works hard for the money. And, loves it that way. So, he sails onto his cool breeze. Debate, and, conquer. Debate, and, conquer. Debate, and, conquer. An easy win!

As Marcus continues on, Cheri begins to think upon the prior night's conversation with her Mother. And that simple answer that she gave for the reason that she, and her Father gave up on all of those years together. Why they were no longer. Then, at once her mind began to wonder upon all the many, petty conversations she, and, Marcus seemed to be having lately. This destructive, war of words that had crept into their engagement. All of those unpleasant interludes. Examination having been said, and, done, "why?" was always the looming question. She sighs, "Why?"

"Well, my friend," Marcus interrupts, not having missed a beat, as he was still quite involved with his telephone conversation, "this victory should give you that champagne feeling all the way home, with an added bonus for the kids." They laugh, and then he mutters something else in butch-man speak that Cheri no longer desires to listen to. "Thank you Frank," Marcus starts in again, "I'll speak with you as we wrap this this whole thing up ,on Thursday."

Shifting interests, he glances over to Cheri's direction. This sweet face that has graced his coveted presence for so many years. He recalls to mind a series of their firsts. Their first glance, first dance, first kiss. The first time he had ever introduced a meaningful female to his mother, his beloved parents. And, so soon into their relationship. Their first date, where he looked at her that way, vowing to make an honest woman of her some day. The night that he did. It made his heart sail to remember these moments that were special to his life. He had developed a keen affection for her. There was just something about her way that forced his hand in that manner. She was exceptional to him. And, though most days he kept this close chested, he new it. Didn't even mind allowing it to shine through on occasion. She deserved it, he confirmed.

"You ready to go?" He fmally confessed through the gritted teeth of his hard won, and, well worn articulation. "I'd like to be early. And, I know how you like to be in time, and, not on time. Well, I need this to go well tonight. So, do you think that you can do that for me?" Then, in notice of the lack of response on Cheri's part, due to her distraction. "Cheri?"

Though thus occupied, Cheri could feel the shift in the energy field. The shield of business having gone down. Otherwise absorbed, and, not at all thrown, Cheri continues on until the appropriate intro resolutes into her sphere. Her way. Tidying matters that she would whisper upon his desk, Cheri intended upon being prompt.

"Do you hear me?" He questions her, spinning around for her response. Finding her, nose in book, and, mid groove. Noticeably, he's irritated. "It didn't use to be this way, he concedes while sitting amidst his cold, although modern, office of blue steel tone, with carefully appointed placards, and various awardings earned over time. The array of successfully fought, and, won legal battles stand at impressive attention. The big win being the careful appointment of his bold, and, newly applied Fung Suie. He'd done well for himself Yet, according to Marcus' hmbitions, this was just the beginning. Yes, just one chain in the link to his long sought for legal stardom. A Legal Eagle, according to all potential. Smiling to himself, he focuses, again on Cheri. In his determined pride sits he, in an air of dissipating arrogance. Taking a moment to examine her, he confesses, "This way between us," his heart pronounces, "It didn't used to be. It just didn't used to be." And he remembers.

Yale Law School. He, the scholar amongst his peers .A valedictorian graduate, he could now soar. Flourishing in his field of choice, Law. A dream that grew with every win of his high school debate team. He'd found negotiations a necessary evil in tying together the fraying ends of an unjust world. "How?" was always the question for him. "How?"

That was a time alone, in a new world, a cool fiber optic reach across the country to Cheri, at Stanford, majoring in fine arts, and, medical science, where she too was flourishing at the top of her class, enjoying her new world, a cool mix of New York, and, bayside that she completely felt at home with. Also thlfilling her role as first born. Bringing her father, who coached her through to scholarship, great pride. She rather enjoyed her time away from the patronage of that hard, busy city. This Northern California just seemed to have a pace that she could sing to, keep pace to, mature in. All of the known tools with which she could find herself All of, or, in part, the dream her father had in mind for her. Upwards of 3,000 miles of space in between this boy, and his teamed pride and joy. Yes, 3,000 miles of space in between him, and, their going steady. "Whew!" was his steady comment. Marcus, on the other hand, had other plans. Seeming incomplete without her, he swore to make a life of this time apart. And, one that her father could approve of "Cheri," he snaps out loud, finally, pulled back from his daydream memoir again into reality. Cheri, engrossed in her hold on intermission, her state of wait, doesn't hear him at all. "All these years, and, she can't get this right. Why can't she be on time with me?" He steams. "Cheri!" He barks out again, slowing his march to a saunter on his approach to her. There he stands, fuming, breathing, fuming, breathing. Cheri, still basking in the malaise of her time-flown occupation, senses his shadow which pipes to a finish upon her as it lands upon her. She glances up brilliantly, and, rests her eyes upon one, annoyed man.

Cheri, quite pleased that his attention, finally has turned to her, flashes that award winning smile of hers. Marcus deflects. Innocently, she removes one of her i-pod ear pieces from her ear to take him in. "Things going well?" She charms. "Must you always have those things on?" He disgusts, as she immediately uncorks the other earpiece from her ear to ready her attention for all that he has to say. "apologies, Marcus.

It's just that you know how I like to keep myself well employed while you are otherwise involved" She repents. "Well built, Cheri. It's well built." He insists. "Indeed." He huffs to himself. For well built she was not. Not yet. Why this gypsy sitting before him right now is nothing of the young lady he saw off to be scholarly, and, thus wise, highly educated. Something was changed in her that had not quite registered to him until now. "Well, she had changed, and, so had he." He resigns. "When are you going to understand that you're too old to go around like this?" He starts in again, heavy with disapproval. "well now, it seems to me that we are past all of the pleasantries. Now, you want to tell me what's really eating at you?" She implies. Marcus is silent. Cheri lets out a heavy sigh through pursed lips while Marcus stands before her, heavy with demand. "Marcus, please don't start." She insists. "Well, then help me with something right through here." He advances. "You're an artist, yes. But, you're a woman too, Cheri. Aside from that, you're my woman. I'm telling you, I'm pulling for higher levels. I'm going to need your presence in representation of me, and you've got to stop fighting me every step of the way." He matter of facts. "I mean it." He concludes with demand. "Well, isn't this something." She defends in thought. "Well, this is the face off." She concluded. And, the two worlds did collide. "Gee, this East vs. West thing, when I'm from the East is indeed not working. Never did." She continues. "I remember it so differently" Cheri recollects.

"Perhaps, Marcus, if you spoke it to me, not at me, it might register. Try it, it just might work." She finally manages. "Clearly, it is everything, Cheri." He decides to surface. "The earphones, the clothes, I mean my goodness, the fact that you'd rather walk here, smelling like city streets than to catch some other dignified mode of transportation is beyond me to be quite frank, and, I'm tired of it."

"This is new." She thought. "I suppose it wouldn't be big enough of you simply to agree that we happen to see things differently. She offers. "Close, but no cigar." He returns. "This is what I've come to understand." He sets up, and, then continues with, "Though our philosophies might be different, our business sense has to be right on point. I want you to be there with me when I really make something of this dream that we've put together. Believe me when I tell you I like you, I even love you, but, I can't build a life like this." On her heart, she remembers far more than their recent, rather fervorernt debates. She notes her privilege of his tenderness, and, the letters he would write faithfully during his days at Yale. Carefully scripted, and, not just of his feelings for her, or, of his achievements, he would write also of his plans for the two of them. Elaborate blueprints of a life together. And, how her father agreed upon his ideas about life. "Why that kid has the meat, and, the heart of it." Her Father was known to have said on more than one occasion. Well, she could bask in the knowledge of that, yet, looking at the two of them now, she had to concede that it was a far cry from what they have had in times past. Not at all pleased with his tone, or his manner, she takes a moment to ingest all of this before her right here. Would they survive this trial, so far in to the engagement? Would they really make it, unlike her father, and, mother, as a married couple? Was he really the man she would play her life with? Though trivial, and, dabbler at first glance, it was fitting for a person of her stature, and, breeding to take a closer look at the weightier matters of this lifelong contract. She studies him a moment, and, then, decides to speak. "Firstly, I feel the need to share with you my surprise with the position that you've chosen to take with me. More than that, you're forcing me to defend who I am, and, especially to you. I'm taken aback, and, quite frustrated with the way things have been going as well, if you don't mind me being so frank." She finally got out.

He takes this in, as the only noticeable feature behind her shades is her brilliant smile. Skin deep in his grimace, he gazes upon her until it fades into one, stiff flat line of defense. He braces for the war, however, litigator at heart, he decides that it is best to, as well, take the high road, and, counter. "Look, now is not the time to mix words in the fashion I foresee this going. Would you please, turn the music off, go freshen up, and, for God's sake, take that ridiculous thing off of your head. This is a corporate dinner I'm leading here. You know this." he attempts. "Nice try, Marcus. You'll do better next time. "She dryly curts. "It's from India, it's called a Sari." She comments, referring to the fabric of head piece crowning her. "I'd hoped you'd be better able to appreciate your own kind." She touches. Stroke in tow, she rises, and, saunters off to fulfill this awfully urgent request. Marcus, not sure whether to be charmed, or enraged at her adorable production. Unprovoked, he turns to his desk, gathering mental notes for the nights events, as the world continues to flow outside of his picture-book window.

Ritz a La Carte!

Arriving in high style, as the quality of life that they had built afforded them the wealth of such luxury as this, they make approach, turning into the valet, while Cheri takes a moment to apply some finishing touches to her make up, and, Marcus can be found polishing off some final, mental notes, taking full advantage of his pre-meeting breath exercises, along with his hopes, and, positive affinnations. It's a jet set life style that they have become accustomed to. Zipping in here, zapping off there. Making the cut, the build, the set, and, staring over again. As partners, he hardly concerned himself with their semi-public, heated disputing, as they could both agree that this grand life they were fighting for, this life of wealth, and, of privilege far outweighed any technical difficulty that they could possibly ever conceive. So, they gather themselves, step on to the scene, meet, and, greet their party, and prepare for an exquisite evening of dollar, and, dinning.

The scene is set with tasteful appointments, as decadent entrée, the hum, and, percolation of pleasant conversation, as, the cheer of laughter rise above the clinks and murmurs of the restaurant atmosphere and, symphony fill the event with an elegant ambiance. This intimate group of business palls are indeed enjoying the evening. They are a table of six, Jacob, and, Liz Bernstein, Warren, and Tasha Potter, and, of course, Marcus, and, Cheri. The group has been together three years, and are already an established team of revenue revolutionists. They lived for the risk, loved for the accomplish, invite the challenge. Money-making moguls they are, intent upon amassing wealth, and, fortune in the combine of their mastered fields. A secret society of legitimate swanks on the rise, stars of the advantaged, proficients of profit. The game was exclusive, and, for the few. They were in it to win. Without question, there was a hunger far more alluring than anything that could be satisfied by that table. This night, in a world where only the strong survive, they realized war.

"Now I see why you've been on such a winning streak. You're a mad man, Marcus. Do you ever sleep?" Warren peaks. "With money flowing, and, a world to build, I beg you not." Marcus humorously curts. "Really, He's been the same since college." Jacob interjects. "We used to call him 'Hype.' He profounds the hyper-focus." "that's right, I'll take a rest. It's called the higher living, and, early retirement." Marcus indulges. They toast, sharing in their ironic laughter, as warren celebrates. "I have no beef with that!" A roar of response is heard from the table, as Marcus, rises from the table, and, again, lifts his glass. "On that note," he introduces, "I'd like to make another toast, as it is in order." He dominates his glass. "To happiness, wealth, fuffillment   He builds. "And, The Carte Blanch benefits of a Free Enterprise!" Jacob heralds. There is a rush of applause, as this starting line up toasts to a pinnacled fhture of high times, rejoicing, and, joviality. They tinkle, and, coo, tinkle, and, coo, tinkle, and, coo. Toasting at the height of the evening. And, underneath the cloak of night, they dance even with the stars. Bravo.

Yes, the group had been intimate for some years. A history rich with good times, and, high flying fellow feelings. They were all high school, if not college sweethearts. A rising elite all their own. Though Marcus and Cheri had yet to become legally official, the group hadn't at all lost step. Not missed a beat. The support was outstanding, not uncommon to a society of sprightly generationaliers accustomed to success. They had a deep love, and, an even deeper loyalty to one another as a whole, and, individually, and, this era of difficulty with which they were being allowed to express would not soon be allowed to succeed. Not if they could manage it. For, they were the "dream team." Why spoil a good thing?

Nights on the town, a power meal here and there, and, the equity just became liquid. They were famous for it. "Speaking of money," Marcus introduces, "Any thoughts on the Intium Stock?" "You couldn't have touched on that at a better time. It is ticking." Warren placates, laughing, and, toasting in agreement. "I don't know about you two, but I'm moving my shares over to Nortex. Brand new company, very, promising.

Cheri is bored to tears. By default she listens in on the female banter. "well, that was Lisbon." Liz bubbles. "Tasha, you must tell me about Paris." She insists. "I don't quite think there are words that could describe the time we had there." Tasha begins. "The food, the couture, the ambiance. Well, it's intoxicating. I might have to e-mail you some keepsakes." She assures. "Wonderful." Liz concurs. Now, twasn't that Cheri didn't like her friends, or her life. It's just that in many different levels, and, in many different ways they had grown apart, were no longer compatible, nor her cup of tea. They paddled, and, babbled in what seemed to her to be petty, and, ninny-nanny. They seemed to live off of the high while doing nothing for themselves. Not at all the life that she wanted for herself "I mean, really, is Marcus going to lead this popcycle stand, or what?" She thought on the average occasion. "Are we to become just like them? Or is there something phenomenal that I am to expect in his plans for our future?" There always seemed to be. Despite his pompous air, Marcus was a wonderful man, and a sweetheart of a provider. He always did have this way of pulling through with a surprise ending at the conclusion of it all. She loved that, and she did have a deep affection for her group of fellows, so, instead of performing her own brand of ninny-nannying, she decides to make a concerted effort to pull a surprise ending all her own. "Did you pick up any art while you were there? You know how culture is my major theme. I've always understood it to be exquisite." Cheri embarks. "No, I don't believe so, as they would say." Tasha offers. "There was so much to see, and do, I guess I over looked much of what would be considered the great art of Paris." She admits. "See, that's exactly what I'm talking about." She frustrates. "Just what did she set out to accomplish there?" She suspicions. Exactly what there to do in Paris but view art? Dig for truffles?" She agonies. "What potato truck did she drop off of?" "Well, there you have it, a legitimate reason for you and warren to go back." Liz enthuses. "Okay I gotta get some air in between me, and, these space cadets." She thinks, and, then offers, "I wonder what it would be like to go alone?" Marcus overhears, and; combats, "What on earth would possess you to think a thing like that? It's just not okay. It's just not okay." He argues. The table's focus instantaneously zones in on Cheri, who is not at all enthused by this new current in the flow of the energy as Marcus' harsh tone has pricked the attention of everyone at the table. Cheri adjust to mask her discomfort, and readies herself for response. "I think it healthy for one to explore the adventure-filled world on one's own before one is no longer singularly obligated." She finally mates to a statement. "So what you're saying is that I need to go to Paris for adventure?" He buffles. "I said I need to go. I'd never presume to know what you would find adventurous." She sloughs off. "Well, after 8 years, I'd think you'd have presumed all over that by now." He wickedly cutes on a fully arrogant harrumph. Cheri is caught off guard by the subtext. Marcus continues. "I mean, why would you look outside about something that is clearly an inside issue?" Cheri feels cornered. She has received this smart-alice, and, cynical questioning in private, but she was not going to be hospitable to, nor invite this public display of their rift. "What, was this to be come a regular fiasco?" She thought. "Well, It might not be as deep as your implication, Marcus. However, if you feel differently, I'm sure we can talk about this later." She steeply hints.

The two face off "This is ridiculous." They both thought as they both trailed onto their private veins. Once, a Power Couple, now they were just a hoot, and, a holler, as the remaining party quickly takes side, and, snuffs any, and, all surfacing response. The evening is never quite the same, as the air goes dead silent, and, all that can be heard is the happy conversation between the enthusiastic clinking of the pleasant china.

Showdown at Sundown

Marcus , and, Cheri continue to disagree to the side, as they wait for the valet. Cheri is livid. She expects this contest in the battle for her dignity to remain private, and, she's not moving space until her tents are agreed upon. Finally, he has made her a public spectacle, and foolish to look upon. As she won that round, she was not about to loose this one either. "What in the world was that?" She begins. "The better question being, what is up with your awfully stank behavior lately?" She torts. "What's up?' "Stank?' What's up with your depleting vocabulary lately? I'll continue to remark it glorified, dignified, creative even." He smirks. This was it for Cheri, and, yet not at all what she wanted. She'd had enough of the secret, and, unsavory bouts of spoken war fare, but to make her a public riot, and to regard their relationship as some discarded sideshow was absolutely enough of what she would tolerate no further. She could tolerate the arrogance, but he'd grown obnoxious with it. It was disgusting, and, distasteful to sec what money, and wealth had done to him. She grew evermore concerned with what the world thought, or how they would receive him. She had high hopes for the both of them. But, recently, she could only find concern for his well being. Was this what he wanted, after all of this building? For her to fade into the background like some delicate piece of artwork? She was not going to live this! Not one moment of it. After so many fights had been won, Cheri was not about slip away into some existence contrary to her nature. This slaying of her spirit, after she'd triumphed all that he'd thrown her way, was not to be. Not to be. Not to be. Not.

"What is wrong with you, lately? If this is what moving up in the world does to you, I really think you should quit while you're ahead, don't you?"

She stands. " Oh, don't do that again. Dare to be broad, Cheri. Isn't that argument stale to you already?" He scoffs. "No, arguing is stale to me, already." She counters. "Listen, my growth as a person is par for the course It doesn't mean that I have forgotten myself" He relates. "That may be so, but, going the extra mile to become a big shot, corporate jerk when I yield beneath my self to support you, certainly says that you have forgotten me!" She steams. "Cheri, please grow up. I'm tired of carrying you to the end zone, if you know what I mean. And, your weird ways are trying my nerves these days." He barks off with sigh. "Well, I'm tired of your pompous nonsense!" She barks back. "And to think, I trusted you with my inward workings, and, deeper feelings. My struggles, and, my triumphs. And, you lay them bare for public display. I'm insulted to my core with your treachery, and, betrayal. How do you expect me to be this deeply in love, while being that severely humiliated? Do you expect me to have any self respect? I don't understand you. I don't understand!" Marcus gathers his face, and, collecting his feelings, he decides to express himself. "First of all, I have no clue as to where you're coming from. It's way left field. Secondly, for many reasons I haven't the slightest inclination to retract a thing. As I have stated, this relationship has taken many turns that I've neither expected, nor enjoyed. I think it's time that were, honest about that, and, time that I'm honest with you whenever, however, come whatever. I'm serious."

This was a side of him that was not going to sit well with her. If she were a cat, and, she would have chosen a panther, she would have leapt at him. She'd had enough of the behind the scenes, was he also to criticize her in public, ruining the societal image she'd worked so well with to develop, and, maintain? "No!" She determined. She would not be destroyed this way. So, with full on frontal attack, she finally deliberates, "Marcus, I'm not going to pretend that this is okay. I'm just not. IT you intend upon making me a public mockery atop of our private rounds, I'll blaze a trail to your face, and, let you know, first hand that I'll not entertain such a cruel ego!" Stunned, Marcus stares, intrigued by this fresh tempest that has just blown in. Not since the returned from Stanford had he seen such a power in her. He was awed, amazed, terrified, turned on a little even. But she would not take this good man down, not this one. So, with machismo he'd not experienced before, he rebuttals, "Woman, I'm going to say this once, and, not twice. Tis I that lifeblood of this relationship, not you. If you think I'm going to lay by the wayside in the face of this level of ingratitude, you're mad. Never will I put up with some hysterical woman who is simply because she is not. You've got to keep up, and, I mean you've really got to do it. If you don't," he threatens, "I will go to extreme measures. I promise you."

This was the straw that provoked her spirit. The constant of bickering, and, threat, bickering, and, threat, bickering, and, threat. "Marcus, we arc not going to survive this. If you are determined to speaking to me in this manner, not backing down for the sake of your self conceit; if your level of importance is so great that you cannot consider me one moment in your shining hour of looking out for number one, I tell you this engagement will not carry through. Not one inlding of a measurement! Mark my words." Marcus grew more indignant with each inflection of her resplendent sagaciousy. He could feel the tide turning, yet he did nothing with it, nor anything about it. Unsure of which direction the lead would exist, he merely paused, bobbing in the subsisting tide, glaring at her with a hate for having been put in this position. Having no words for the helplessness that he'd brought upon himself, he remained silent for what would read an eternity. Grossly irritated, and, vengeful, Cheri took the wrong clue, for he had not found the point on which to stand, and, she took in this hint more completely than his one to recommence. Irate, and, refusing to be beneath that which she is, and not at all sorry for the fuct that that she refuses to apologize for it, she removes her engagement ring, and, threatens him back with a gesture to pitch, and, "A boy you are, and, a boy you will be always as long as you refuse the maturation of my sensibilities. Just what did you expect me to do, disappear into the oblivion, while you bask in your glory? No! I shall not sink quietly into this night while you know my value not! I shall rise as the phoenix, while you sink like the Titanic, so you can praise me some also. Also! Yes, I plan to chuck your term of endearment, and, had hoped that you would've caught my drift by now. Because if this is all I know, or, can expect from you, I don't want it!"

She, in her full glory does indicate her desire to chuck the glorified point of light at him, gauphunphing in reprise, as he is fully taken aback at this display of rebelliousness on her part. He, too, is irate, furious as he now stands powerless to her disgust, and, public vexation. They were both in the wrong by now, only, Cheri felt justified in the validity of its point, its ugliness. That he should never have performed that public execution, the group eradication of her delicate ideas, that surfaced only to be slayed by friends under the influence, his. Finally, grasping his station, he braces for this new undertaking; winning her back from the abyss of personal insult. Sure, he'd been hard to put up with for an eternal stint. He'd always sharpened his skills of debate against her great mind. Without regretful consideration, It only came natural to measure the intriguing, though adolescent queries, theories, and, trials that he wished to expand upon, and, mature. In retrospect, he could see how pushing the personal note could have been a wrong turn, but, he was only trying to grow her. Take her mind to new places with him where he could not go with anyone else. Like a trialsome litigation, in retrospect, he could see how cluing her in from time to time would have been a wiser choice than the ones he had made. In retrospect, He was just plain wrong. He knows now, that if he does not play this pivotal card right, he could loose her.

So, in preparation of the greatest legal battle of his young career, Marcus motions in the hope of no objection. "Cheri, really, I'm not fmding a need to be so violent in exchange with one another, he appeals. "Why do you then?" She grants, still steaming from the evening's scandal. "Allow me to fmish," he offers, " I won't." "I'm telling you Marcus Erickson, If these words don't move mountains, I'll not make one more move with you. Not one more." She warns. "Why must you arrange things in this manner, putting things in term I might not survive?" He starts. "Oh, you'll survive. You'll survive, or I'm out." Cheri insists. "Cheri, come on." He contests. "I don't think you understand, Marcus. After all the threat, and, personal violence to my character, and I mean your words really hurt. After all of the personal insult. I mean it was enough behind closed doors, but, tonight, Marcus, tonight was really something. To bring it to our public life?" "Now wait here, "he protests. "No, I won't." She opposes. "I mean, in all your glory, you shot me down!" Marcus measures, and, is silent., "To make me feel a fool, is that your aim?" She seethes. "No, I   He begins. "To cast me as your jesting tool?" "No..." He secures. "What are you jealous Marcus?" Marcus guards hinisell aghast, with an expression that reads her revelation to be an exposure, or a lie. "I mean, I have so many questions you've not the answers to. So, why even bother? Why include me in your pageantry, and in this masquerade recently created for yourself if in fact I do not matter?" Marcus is still silent. "Don't, don't poo-poo me away with your standard, lawyer me, give me a reason to believe in you again. Come on, give me your direct, don't get shy on me now, hit me with it. You are subpoenaed, and, baby, I am ready for you!"

Marcus, taken aback, and, not ready for this fire, takes a deep breath, and, readies himself for the dance of his life. "Woman, Cheri, I haven't the heart to hurt you anymore than what the night has already exposed. What I want you to remember in all of this is my deep concern for you. I am in a caring position when it comes to your affections, and, your attention." Cheri listens. "I don't want to loose what we've built, so, I will be mild. You do mean everything to me. "What it is," he sighs, "is that I'm not feeling the mix of our paths lately. We should be parallel, harmonious, tandem even. Honnie, I can't put my finger on it, but, we're asque, and, I don't want it like this." Cheri, formed, and, made in this moment of ironic delivery, flashes with a made up mind. Both unconvinced, and, dissatisfied with his tired defense, and, explanation, she steps forward with something to say. Coolly she proceeds. "Marcus, I've seen your best, and, that wasn't it. If that is all I am worth to you, I'm going to have to revamp, and, rethink a thing or two, because I don't like it. I often think of how my father would respond having knowledge of our theatrics. And, you know what he would say?" She steps a breath's hair into his face, removes her engagement band, and, looking him dead in the eye, takes his hand ever so carefully to make the point, and, drops the ring on to his bear palm, confessing, "No more, thanks."

She begins to move away, he goes to stop her. "Excuse me?" He alerts. This turn he neither expected, nor would he live down sans a real fight to win back her affections. Anything would be better than this cold, unpronounceable air about her. "Cheri, if you have a point to make, trust that there is a better one to be had." He reasons.

"Just what do you have in mind?" Her ultimatums, giving him a strong sense of the all too obvious fact that he had better brush up on his basic, court-dry etiquette, or, be held in stiff contempt of her court. "Listen, Cheri, you can't bob, and, weave with me through extremes like this. We're in love. And, sure, lately we've beaten off the well known path, but I thought that we had a kindred I could call upon, count on this empty, though overcrowded, lackluster for true love, amongst this space cadet central here. Now, I do perform well on my own, Cheri, however, I don't get far without you. You know this. I thank you for gracing my growth pains. Please don't walk off like this."

"Not bad." She tastes, as she rolls it upon her pallet, like a savory sample of wine. "But your 'I love you's' are lacking lately, Marcus. I mean, really, your spar far out finesses any touch you could improve upon." Marcus, in all the years he learned to be together, his mouth agape. She walks off to hale a taxi. "Wait, wait, wait! Slow this down. I think we got way too hot a little too fast." Yet there is no stopping her. "No, I think we've hit our peak, Marcus." She concedes. "I think, in this pivotal moment, right now, we ought to be thankful that we caught it. I know that I am." She continues to walk off toward her costly transportation. As the valet pulls up, Marcus is in a quantum's leap. Stuck right on the proverb. He's not familiar, nor has he ever gotten acquainted with this instinct in her. This trigger that walks off. And means it. "Sir." The valet calls out. "Cheri, wait a minute!" He scuffles out after her, having not even noticed the arrival of his vehicle, or the steward in its charge.

Never has he felt as powerless as this. He flashes back to the moment right before the announcement was made, unknowingly regarding himself, for the ultimate victor of the regional, scholastic, all around debate held in Baltimore, Maryland, at Harvard University. What was he to do? Pull the all too unpopular move with the crying game? Stand in his druthers, adamant, and, consolingly in the skeleton of his machismo? He decides to move. "Cheri!" He masters into the air, sprinting in full pursuit.

Cheri, stepping, in full steam. Never before had she witnessed such a lifeless response to such a lifelong procession. "I mean," she garphumphs, "are we to dance like this throughout all of our engagement, and, marriage? Our life?" No! "Marcus, I've heard enough! I'm going home." She gestures into the air with the flick of her wrist, calling behind herself from the sing of her mane. "Keep it!."

"Will you just wait?" he insists, his voice cracking with hot demand, and, cry, as his life is fading away into the perspective. The valet calls again. "Sir, pleas; I have many people." "One moment." He chops at the man, as he hurries of in a dash toward Cheri, who has already hailed a cab. Cheri!" He tears into the aft. "You can't! You simply can'f' He chokes out as he arrives at the cab door.

"Marcus, hailing all sanity, I don't know what to make of this! You love me, you hate me, you love me, you hate me, you love me, you hate me. I don't know the heads from the tails of this relationship anymore! And, you know what's more? I don't like you.. .A LOT!" She closes the cab door. "Cheri, be reasonable. I love you!" She gives him a dry look. "I might be blind to a few things Marcus, but I'm no fool." "Cheri, come on!" "Step on it!" She finally barks out to the cab driver. He does.

The car speeds off into the night, as Marcus is left standing in the clouds of exhaust. Their once upon a time, now a deserted oasis.

M4ty Out!

After an exciting night out, home was just what Cheri needed. So, she sauntered on through the entryway of her Mother's brownstone, beyond the living room, and into her private quarters. Where. she could be at peace. Where she could be at, best. Where, she could be, honest.

It was in here that the walls were decorated with the spectrum of anger fits, screaming spells, and, frustration tirades fresh from any of her recent, and, unsuccessful conversations with Marcus that left her in misery, but, not defeat. Her father would say that she should have payed clear attention to the signs, and, have gotten out with full revelation. "But, then again, " he would sigh, "a woman I am not, and, a woman's heart I do not have." Then, he would smile, and, say something else wise, or witty. Leaving her to nibble upon thought. It was in here where she kept her meticulous collections. Art-inspired philanthropies, that garnished her surroundings, giving her solace at the fact that she had such private wisdom, that she could turn to on a blue page, and, from within her deepest melancholy, gain the power to inspire, or, idea. T'was here, indeed, that Cheri could cry.

She lies awake, staring at the ceiling, combing through the past 8 years of her life. Tossing, and, turning. Tossing, and, turning. Tossing, and, turning. Throughout the night until the morning, as she sorts, purges, and, cancels her bertoval out of existence. Throughout this night, we are a witness to the various stages of her metamorphosis from anger, to crippling heartache, to depression. We view the intercepts of her life (photos, awards, certificates, etc.), until the morning. Finally the phone rings. She allows the service to pick up. "Hey, Cheri. This is Mai. I was wondering if you could bring my Bach CD back tonight. Thanks." Cheri references the time. It's 4:45pm.

She has exhausted every connection to, and, dedication for, her currently, past honored "high life." Her false friends, her staged performances, and, her altogether, overly glorified existence. Their lifestyle of the "gods" no longer appealed to her, as she was no longer interested in its brass ring. She no longer craved this postulated rostrum that they had presumed upon themselves. And, yet, her pulse of life keeps pounding, and, as she finally arouses from this epiphany, she is startled to the all too true reality, "Oh my god! Work!"

Cheri darts out of bed, and, scrambles to get ready for the evening.

You Gotta Sonata!

Cheri stands backstage before the theatre mirror. A reflection that she cannot see. Finally, Cheri takes off her shades, and, for the first time, we see that she is blind. From the time of her early childhood, Cheri has always been exceptional. Excelling in maths, sciences, and, the arts. All of the major areas that would mark her for early genius. Then, one day, at about the age of 8, by way of some uncanny happenstance, Cheri simply lost sight. Having to take on a new life ruled by the esthetic. Doctors, and, specialists alike, were absolutely baffled. And, her mother was completely devastated. Adjustment was a must, as her father worked with her to accustom his daughter to this new extension on existence. Learning first himself, and, then walking her through the brail. Sighting her visual memory to accept, and, master this new world of negative vision. Training her muscular, and, radial responses, so, that she would be able to conquer any know terrain. The world was hers to have. A la carte, and, a Ia mode. Compliments of daddy!

If ever there has been a moment of more importance. Her life, until now only seemed to cancel out in stages where she needed levels. Sure, Marcus was difficult, but, not impossible, and certainly not unworthy of her proper love, If only the balance in understanding could swing her way sometime. Why he never seemed to volunteer this was an outright disillusionment for her. Why he never stopped to think of her when her face would turn that emotional shade of red, while he would infallibly breakdown her character to a ninth of an inch, Metrically dissolving any, and, every moment of triumph that she could possibly attain, pounding her with words whenever she would muster confidence, gratifying himself in the dwarfmg of her character? Why he was so much, and yet nothing all like the man who brought her into this world, and, gave her life? Why he couldn't just be her Prince Charming?

A stage manager calls her into place. A full orchestra is waiting in the wings. The signal is given, and, in one, wave of organized movement, the entire company takes its place. Cheri iii flow, to her concert piano. Positioning herself on her concert bench, she poises her frame, and, places her fingers for ready to play. The conductor mounts his podium, readies his musicians, and, releases the flood of symphonic harmony with one, crisp sweep of his arm.

This for her has been the dream of all dreams. The triumph of all triumphs. Her life's dream. However, Cheri, at the piano, is cooperating with the music, but, not feeling it, not really. She just does not yet feel in tune with this expression that she must keep in time with. It is a wonderful Mozart piece. Concerto No. 20 in A minor. She stifles the personal weight of the day, her called off engagement, the god awful rivalries that led to it, the way these things have thrown off her natural rhythm altogether. Cheri realizes that this overture could very well be a turning point to the soundtrack to her life. She cannot fall apart now, and, she knows it.

She follows the music, as the momentum builds, and, peaks, builds, and, peaks, builds, and, peaks, until finally it crescendos in duet with the lead violinist. Stirred, and, refreshed, the audience explodes in appreciative applause. Cheri, moved to tears, as she has just been completely expressed, and, well spent within this masterpiece of purge. Mourned, and, cleansed of her adolescence, she is thankful to have found new life in her non-combative world.

To Flight!

Sigh. Another fine evening, leaving Cheri exhausted, and, emotionally spent. Collapsing onto her bed. Going through her mail, she brails through a contest for a trip to Paris. She makes a darted move to her computer. Referencing travel sites, she is, for the first time, in what has seemed ages, in wonder, as the voice-activated attachment to her lap top has her in a sphere of charm, grace, and eloquence.

She recalls the previous night's catastrophic events to her dishonor. Her one, bright moment was the revelation for freedom again. She flourished in it. The new air, fresh customs, and spirited souls, culminating in an all around improvement to hers. Her father was never happier, her sister, never so surprised, and, her mother never with a greater sense of pride. And the hope... she wanted that again. Weaving through the fiber optic maze, she found world travel more, and, more irresistible, with the descriptives from her assisted log ever so inviting. An executive decision must be made, so, let it begin with gay Paris!

Packing her bags with great anticipation, she can hardly stand the excitement, as she is about to sneak out of the country. Cheri hadn't had this level of thrill, since she, and, Marcus used to sneak up to her bedroom window to avoid the living room shotgun her father held to show his disapproval of her missing curfew. Brailing her mother on the keyboard, she pops it on to the refrigerator, and, heads for the door. On the way to the airport, she is full of adrenaline. Her life flashes before her, as she is all too well aware that she was encountering her bloom. Her life is about to become very interesting, and, she doesn't want to miss a single, overseas moment of it!

She breathes in a sigh of relief, as she boards, and seats herself on the plane, ready to embark on this new journey. Now 2:00 Am., she's dined, been entertained, and, now settles in for sleep, quite pleased with her secret escape. Her mind does wonder, however, about how her sister will get along without her for a while. Though of the seeing world, she was so vehement with her envy of Cheri that she locked herself out of her father's love, and, her mother's admiration, and so was just as blind, if not more so handicapped. Yes, Cheri, all of the family, really, were well aware of her self imposed, and, ongoing competition with Cheri. Why, they were twins. So, this has been something silly to everyone involved. Though she loved her sister dearly, she was only a mystery, and, an enigma to herself At least she was true to that.

And, mother, what would she think? How will she fare? Why, since father left, Cheri had been the masculine influence in the house. And, for so many year, for this, or, for that mother needed. "Perhaps this is one point of many reasons why sister suffers from envy so." Cheri poises. She found it interesting to note why she kept this riddle to herself Why their relationship should, and, could have taken so many better turns. "Mother, and, I speak about it," she professes, "father, and, I deal with it, why she doesn't trust me with the issues on her heart." She heaves. I guess I'll just leave that to hope, and, prayer." Sigh. It's always been Ramona vs. Towanda.

"Now," she thought, "Father, though he might express a little concern, would root her on. Mostly because it involved her growth, and, development, and, her independence from Marcus. He'd hinted quite a bit, for a while, then, one day, he just mentioned, outright about his desires for her to expand her station, adventure the world, something. But, there was always some other thing with Marcus.

"You mean, after three years of courtship, that young man keeps you only local, uses your relationship to build his life, and, has no other interest than to make money, which includes you according to the wealth of my many years? I don't know how, or why you do it, but you are going to have to get that boy to regard you, I mean really regard you." He was serious. Just woke her up one day. "God, Marcus, why do you have to be so thick-headed?" She protests. "Oh well." She sighs. And, as the plane sails through the high skies, we know she's got a multitude of things on her mind, and, more held to her chest. She indeed will be making some life-changing decisions on this travel-inspired venture. As the plane coasts on, Cheri sets herself to cozy up, close her eyes, and, sail off to sleep.

Finally, the voice of the flight attendant can be heard with the announcement of the final decent. Persons begin to organize their things, returning their tray tables to their upright positions. Cheri fixes her shades, gathers her things, and braces herself for the clean landing. Success!

She takes a moment, while still on the plane to activate her artificial sight. A radio-active, digitized instrument that creates an animation to the world around her. She see by way of an electrical current frequency, which affords her a complete comfort with which to familiarize herself within any environment. Quest ready, she establishes herself amongst the other travelers set for disembarkment. The anticipated charge gives her a rush, as she files on into the terminal.

While making her way through the tenninal, she is knocked by an awfully rude, and, shaded man, who apologizes quickly, asking her where she's going, and, how he can help. He directs her in the way of the public transportation. She picks up track, and, heads off in the direction of the instruction given. Parting with thank you's, and you're welcomes.

On the way to, and, upon being seated upon the train, she, thinks briefly about all that she was leaving behind. Her childhood, when she could see. Her life beyond that, when she couldn't. The contrast of this phenomenal occurrence was overwhelming for her at first. Then, taking on a life of its own, it seemed more natural to her to become descriminant, or, inclusive based upon the elements that she could not see. "My little justice." Her father would call to her affectionately. Then, there was Stanford, and, her time away from all that was regulatory. Sure, it was a variation of her old world, with its rules, and, standards, deadlines, and, curfews, however, like Paris, it was hers. She would make it, indeed, she would make it.

In the air she could feel the energy. The excitement, the exhilaration, the electric charm. The city was animated with thrill, and, enthusiasm. Even the language exploded with sensation, and, delight. Parle-vous frou, frou, frou, nous allon ca tu parle? Je, je, je, jai! So, it sounded to her. Both questions, and, commands bubbled forth with delights, joys, and, pleasures. The very sound of it stirred, electrified, and excited her! Why, the joy of being overseas was almost more than she could bear. But she'd promised herself, "I'm going to make it!" She aflirined with such a conviction. She just had to measure up, and, follow through. Just had to!

As she exit's the taxi, in front of the hotel, she wants to cheer, and, shout, as Paris gives her the impression that they really celebrate, that the festivities are never-ending. The bun is quite an event. She could hardly stand it. Bursting with excitement, she surges her way through the revolving doors, and, on into the hotel lobby. She checks in, addresses her busboy, and, soars up, and, into her room.

The first thing that she desires after such an extended travel is to bathe. So, she opens her travels through Paris with a shower. Cheri can't help but to wash that overstuffed apple out of her hair, as she sloughs away every pain, every insult to her character, and, every plan that didn't go according to her accustomed to. As she steps out of the shower, wraps her towel, applies her robe, she saunters over to the terrace to breath in the night air. A virgin to the culture, and, allure of Paris. Hungry for life, and, open for change, she is ready for Paris, but is Paris ready for her.

Embracing the city, first thing, she declares with her complimentary glass of Champaign, "Why you magnificent city. We'll do well together, for I see you just fme. To the toast of my life!"

As she basks in the warm hue of the European sunset, we know that life for her will never be the same. It can only improve from here. Going up!

Exit, Stage Left

Ahh, Dana, what can be said about her, for now, except that she is Cheri's sister, to date? "Cheri, I needs to talk." She confesses, as she enters Cheri's room only to fmd that she's not there. "Cheri?" She call out again, in the hopes that she is somewhere. Now, Dana, who's been Cheri' s sister all of her life, is no wilting lily. It's been her power to have been so clandestine as far as this. But now she was ready for a true, heart of hearts, down to the baseline, nitty gritty speak. "Cheri where are you?" She hollows, peering around, and, into all of Cheri's usual spaces. Again, and, again, until she concedes with a certainty that Cheri is most certainly not in. "Well, I was going to invite you to breakfast, however, I think that I'll just do it alone, 'cause you're not here, so, I'majust go somewhere 'cause I see you're not here, and, I need to talk to my sister." She confesses. "Do you hear me?" She frustrates. Nearly in tears. "I need you!" She fits, and clomps out of the room with a broken spirit.

Now, its not that Dana is envious of Cheri, it's just that she cannot wrap her mind around the fact of how she got to be the favorite. You see, Cheri has always been "handicapped" in Dana's mind, yet, Cheri has always excelled, and Dana can't understand it. You see, Dana, in her world, is used to being the best at what she does now. When they were younger, it was all Cheri's world. Cheri this, and, Cheri that. Cheri could dance better, Double Dutch better,do hair better. Cheri, Cheri, Cheri! Everything was Cheri. I mean what was Dana, chopped liver, the wicked step sister, a monkey in a cage? Really, what Cheri stopped seeing, and, could no longer do those things, not well anyway, Dana thought that she had it made. She just knew that it would be all about Dane. And, all ABOUT Dana! But, it's not. It's all about Cheri. STILL! It's Cheri's world, and, all Cheri's world, and, she can't stand it! Lord knows she cannot stand it. Man, she can't stand it! "Darn Cheri! I can't stand her!"

And, she really thinks all of this, as she treads her little mighty, tighty way into the kitchen. "I mean, she really cannot cook better than me with her blind self Ijust can't stand it! I'm the one who can see! I'm the one who's flamboyant! I'm the one who's capable! Okay sure, Cheri can do most anything once you explain it, but, you have to explain it!" She baffles. "I, on the other hand, see it, and, do it! I study it. Naturally. It does not have to be explained!" She beleaguers. "I just don't get it! Why?" She almost in tears. "Why can't I get the special attention that I was born to encompass? I know I have it. I know I'm worth it. Why?" Spinning around in all of her drama, she spies the not left from Cheri to her mother., and, snatching it off. "Why the heck dose she always have to steal the show?" As she reads, the devastation sets in slow motion. "Why you little..." full echoed banchi, "Mom, She's done it again!"

A panic attack, and a heart break later, "This isjust like her to up, and hop off to another country. Her life here couldn't have been that bad. Right?" She complains to her mother. "I don't know, honnie," Mona steadies, "She had a pretty bad break up with Marcus the other night." "God, she doesn't tell me anything anymore!" Dana calculates, storming out of the room, leaving Mona to piece the puzzle, and rhyme the riddle. "Well, Robert isn't going to like this." She recognizes. "Cheri, darling, what in all the world are you doing?" Mona addresses, holding the note, and, crossing to the phone.

C'est, La Vie!

Cheri leisures through Paris city streets with the ease of her New York swagger. Like riding a bike, she owns, tames, and, masters this new cadence of Parisian promenade. Why, there is so much to explore. The sidewalk, pastel artists, that don't mind the magnetic stroll that plays through her delicate frame, as she streams through. There are the portrait artists that call out to her for the opportunity to capture her. The fashion boutiques that kindly persons direct her, to where she can be fit to size, blend in, and, express her version of a Ia France!

Cheri dips into the public market. Sampling, and indulging in Parisian fmcries that tantalize her as yet simplistic sensories.

The flower shops draw her by day, that call to hr by fragrance.

The various towns people that call to h her (children, elders, lovers, and, the working class).opportunities that establish the cultural diversity.

Moved by public musicians.

Feeling the dance of the street performers (classic jazz, ballet, freeform).

Finally, she is forced back into the place she left with the ring of her cell phone. She answers. "Hello? Mom.. .yes, I'm fine." She confirms. "Well, I'm glad to hear that. Cheri, you gave us all a start, Honnie. I know you're used to being on your own, but, this is downright outrageous." Mona concerns, amid the traffic of the Big Apple. "A start? Outrageous? Is it because I left a note?" She octaves with laughter. Or, is it that I know longer need a permission slip to take a trip that's got you all in a bunch? Trnst me, I'm fme, ma. I've been independent quite some time now, or, have you forgotten? You gonna' fight me on that too?" Cheri chortles. "Cheri, you're my daughter, I will always fight to keep you secure, and, if it means 'little-girling' you from time to time, then call it like you feel it, but, that's-a what

I'm-a gonna do." She exclaims, waiting for her daughter's next smart to allec. "Mom, for ages, now, I've been my own, grown woman. I'm in my prime, thankfully on my own, and, in the city of romance, well if you aren't cramping my style, I must be crazy too." She jests. "Yea, you know not to get too cute with me, missy. I've got to hop across town, so, I'll let you go. Glad to know that you're safe, my love." End call.

Triumphant with her mother, Cheri takes in the appetizing aroma of a quaint, little, sidewalk café within her immediate. Enchanted, Cheri enters, and, is seated, and begins to study from her language textbook. "Bonjure!" She melodies While continuing to work through the enunciation of the next phrase, she is noticed by a most adorable little girl sealed with her grandmother. Charmed by the struggle, the child giggles, and, coos, giggles, and, coos, giggles, and coos, fmally, joining in on this engaging play on words. "A quell heure est Ia prochain train de Paris?" The little girl sings out the correct pronunciation, while being hastened to a hush by her guardian. Cheri smiles, plasanted in the assistance of such a delightful presence. "A quell heure est Ia prochain train de Paris?" She harmonizes, thoroughly humored in the experience. Holding her place, she tries another one. "Commonts apelle-tell?" She draws out carefully. "km 'apelle Chloe'." The tiny tot chorts out, bursting with explosive tee-hees from under her grandmother's definitively marked, fine line. She reprimands something in correction to the wee one, as Cheri laughs in the excited enrichment. Aglow with humor, they exchange "Merci' s," and, "Adue' s, as Cheri is then brought to the attention of her waitress. It had been am interesting game of verbal Peek-a-boo, but, now, it was time to satis~' her need for nourishment. Cheri is then assisted by her server. "What can I get for you, Madame?" She begins. "Fresh berries, and, cream, pleasc, with thc side of a crepe." She savvies, simmering down from her sonar pitter-pat. "Very well." The waitress corresponds, moving off to right away the order. Cheri resumes her study, and, pronunciation application, only now, An older, silver-headed man catches ear. "Quel age ayes vous? Pouvez parle plus lente. . . lente. . . le..." "Len-te-ment. Pouvez parle plus lentamente?" He sounds out for her in perfect, Latin phonetic. Cheri catches herself in laughter once again. "Merci!" Her happy heart toots in response. "Bo coupe." He finalizes, encouraging her progress, "Very fme, young lady. Very fine! Aihorde!" As, he continues on his way.

Unbenouneed to either of the party is Antoine Diadoux, young, mid twenties, tall, dark, handsome. From wealth, having close family ties to the Queen, Antoine is a natural royal. Yes, he's traveled the world, yet, all of his life, he's lived in France. Ties to his lineage, and, ancestry. On his way to a darker appointment, he spots the café, decides he's got some time, and, chooses to dine. Rounding the entrance, he immediately spots, and, observes with increasing intrigue, as the older gentleman, and, Cheri at their word play, and, exchange. As she continues with the lesson, he assists her with the third, and, most challenging phrase, and pronunciation.

Waving off the martrede'e, Antoine prowls her way, peering with keen interest this move that drove this inward, conscious instinct. "Le matan, le midi, le soir." She rehearses. "Il est midi." "Comment ca va?" He sneaks in, and, commences. "Puis-je voir la carte de yin?" She requests, mistaking him for her server. "Que-est que c'est?" He questions. "Parle vous Ingle's?" She reflects. "Oui, oui." He answers. "I speak English very well." "Good, French to English, excellent! Assist me here." She excites. They read it together. "L'astronomers cherchent du autre mondes de l'universe." "bien, bien." He confirms. "Very good, indeed." He admires, kissing his fisted hand. " I may see you around." "Who are you?" She inquires. Exuding charm, "Did I not say? Good." He rushes off leaving her to wonder. Queried, she baffles off through clenched teeth, "C 'est la vie!"

Post refreshment, Cheri strolls along the country road, pronouncing to herself what she's learned from her language book. Heat, and, debris from the extreme temperature changes on the road, and, coasts, and, sails through the air, revealing Antoine, not far behind. As she continues on, a cat breezes by, startling her. She laughs, calming herself with a quick round from "Aloetta." Antoine, absorbed, and, quite pleasantly aroused by this newest, musical sensation, is in all actuality, entirely intrigued. He measures, and, then seizes the opportunity for capture. But, he's got to get her attention somehow. He gains ground, and, somewhere within the verses, he surprises her by cutting her off, and, completing it. He's got her attention now, and, well uses the advantage. Stepping in front of her, he locks eye contact, and, continues to stroll in front of her, backwards. In his attempt to exchange in the eye-play that must be behind those designer shades, he notices that something is different about her. He doesn't let that stop him, After an awkward moment, finally he speaks. As he snickers a bit. "So," he startles. How is your French coming along?" "Who are you?" She gasps. "Who am I?" Neither one of them shaken. "Yes, who are you?" "L'astronomers cherchent du autre mondes de l'universe?" Snickering. "I am Antoine, and you?" "Oh!" She reveals, and, laughs. "Que-est-ce que c'cst! Commont ca va? Commont alles vous?" Radiating. "Bien, bien. Et tu?" Bustling with amusement, she tills, "Why, I never thought I would encounter you again! This is wonderful! So, really, how are you?" She flashes. "Quite well." He responds. "These introductions are almost always a necessary evil, no?" Finally, she extends the invitation. "I am Cheri." He savors, amused in his admiration, he covers in his sly grin, as he fmally returns the expression, "Indeed, I am Antoine. Charmed."

Into the Wild!

Now, Cheri, not your every buttercup, was turning out to be the choicest pick amongst the spray. The select fare, so far, in the eye of Antoine.

From the time of her youth, she was arrayed with a an allure, an attracting aura that seemed to only surfaced here now, in this uncharted terrain. An innocent attraction. With the essence of honey bees, Gardenias on the wild, sunsets, and, exotic, spring drinks.

She was top of her class, the "coup de tat" in the pinnacle of arenas, the wonder beneficial. Born and bread for greatness, her song played like the supreme aria before Antoine now. As A goddess of the heavens she appeared with her everlasting glow. He must touch it somewhere, somehow. So, he starts in, "Is that of you?" Referring to her package. "Come again?" She whisps, trying to track his reference. "The canvas. Do you mind, I'd like to see." He trepodates, as he helps her to unearth a modest, hand sketched portrait of herself. He admires. "Nice, however, I can do better." He admits, for, he had an affinity for the arts of varied sorts, particularly the class of frameworks.

"Should I take you seriously?" She inquisits. "Completely." He cavaliers, beaming, in his thousand watts. Fortunately, for him, and, to her surprise, she falls into his play. She is humored, and, can't resist the surface, as it reviews with cracked, and, then knowing smile. Antoine cannot resist. And, as he returns the precious work of art, Antoine, and, Cheri exchange touch by palm. Cheri cannot help, but, to meet with enchantment. And, as their encounter completes its cycle, Cheri cannot escape his self-imposed ecstasy.; And, as she grabs hold of his wrist, she catches hold of his crested, charmed bracelet. "Are you free this evening?" He distracts. And, as he recoils his hand, the crash of the charms evokes a flashback. She recollects the shady character she bumped into at the airport. Close-flash, and, slow motion in on the sound of his identical, crested bracelet.

"Well?" Cheri, being called back into real-time, by Antoine. "Perhaps" She manages, clearing her throat. "Well, if you appreciate the work of true artists, you might want to make your way over to La Resitance this evening." "Sounds interesting..." She considers, clearing her throat once more. "Perhaps." She closes. "Well, if you need me for anything he holds out to her a card from the same hand wearing the crested, charmed bracelet. She notices its meldic chime. "Call me."

As Cheri cannot see, she is clueless to this silent gesture, as his hand hangs, in the air, mid suspension, for what seems to be an endless hold. The delay, by now noticeable by the both of them, creates a bated awkwardness that causes the two of them to share the same pace, same, breath, same dimention. This beat fades into a panted pause, as realities natural pace blends into this just born rhythm.

"Please. Hello?" He fmally lures, almost whistling , and snapping his fmgers. "Cheri?" He melodies to get her attention. "Excuse me?" She snaps into play. "Tonight, if you'd like to." He refers, reintroducing the same, silent gesture, this time with a more forward approach. He takes his hand, and, guides it to touch. Careful, as his aim is, unintrudingly, for her hand.

Making contact, he finds success, only in startling her. "Oh, my God! What are you.. .what is this?" She cries, recoiling, and, covering, so as not to uncover her secret. "My card, please. I'm merely offering you my card. Please take it." "Oh, your card!" She says, gasping for a good breath. "Oh, my God! Please excuse. Thank you."

Antoine, on track of her allure, is held to position. Charmed, he is still very attracted, fascinated, and, amused all at the same time. Caught, he seriously desires to uncover this mystery of his attraction. To bounty this fresh unknown. To take possession of this object of unexpected passion. Ready, or, not, he was in pursuit. On he hunt for something he could not quite put a fmger on, yet well aware of the fact that something worth exploring was right before him. A sensation he determined to acquaint himself with.

Eureka! As ecstasy surfaces, and, she hesitantly, but decidedly accepts his offer. "Your card. Oh, thank you." She receipts. "Maybe tonight?" He beckons. "Perhaps." She confinns, with a fmal clearing of her throat. They smile.

"I'll see you tonight. Au'revoir.." He finesses. "Perhaps." She taunts. With that, they're offi Clearly, the two of them are mutually intrigued. In his expression of it, Antoine tosses a coin into the air. Cheri, who positions herself for demarcation, can, again, hear the distinctive chime of his crested bracelet, with the looming coin balancing their delicate arrival.

Back in time, at the café, where the two of them met, people are eating, and, life is au cache'. A body washes up to the water' s edge. Someone spots it, and, screams out. On his right wrist, he spots the same, crested charm as Antoine, and, as the man at the airport. As the waves fondle the coin, we are haunted by its dull chime.

Night Fever!

Paris, city streets were a welcomed change from the country sideways. The action infectious, The lights, free, and, the people, oh, so refreshing!

Cheri walks right in amongst the street vendors, sampling fruits, sweets, walnuts. All that they had to supply!

Antoine, miles away, is checking his watch, and is on the phone.

Cheri, waltzes into a quaint, little boutique. She likes the feel. Putting away her sight stick, to summons, gesturing into the air for assistance. A floor clerk approaches.

"May I help you?" She bubbles. "Yes, I'd like something in yellow." She enters. She figured that suck a cheery color would be just the right note to start on. She remembered that she love the vibrance! It went well with the sunshine. She used to love to see the light bounce from the concrete, to her attire, and, strait back to the sun. She loved the play. She loved the joy. She loved the sheer delight of it all! One of her fondest memories of sight was the color yellow.

Antoine liked the open air of the countryside, where he was awaiting the arrival of a package. He toted along with him the complete packaging of his stealthily correct attaché' case. He loved to broad, open space where he could think. Where he could become. Where he could be. It was the in this open space that deal of a lifetime would indeed go through. So, there he stood, in this wide, open space, the wind blowing in, past, and, around. In his wait, he grows impatient. "Come on." he beckons.

As the expectant arrives, Antoine is refreshed. The carrier has with him many, well disguised goods. "Good, Finally." He cheers, for Antoine was not the dark type, though he did love a good, deep-hued game. "Get in." Announce the driver, a truly, dark-typed character. Chestnut hair, gaunt features. Not at all a woman's dream. Why, with his greased skin, and, pocked face, he could put a chill through he meanest of adversaries. Serious about his business, he again, insisted, "Get in."

Antoine takes a moment for breath. And, gets in. "You got what I need?" He jutted. Antoine refers to case. "There's more."

Back at the boutique, Cheri is in various stages of dress in the fitting room. She tries on for size, tries on for size, tries on for size, and, finally, she is glorious!

Meanwhile, at the meeting place for Antoine's exchange. Antoine opens his case to reveal hard, cold cash. He accepts the payment, and, the exchange is made. Dark, and, cold is the mood.

Otherwise, at the boutique, Cheri is engaged in her cash exchange for the goods she has just purchased. She basks, and, exit's the store.

At that moment, Antoine inspects, and, examines the quality of his exchange. Antoine, and, expectant have successfully made the exchange. They shake hands, and, get into car. His return awaits.

By this time, Cheri dashes into her hotel., Carrying her goods. Glowing with package, she ascends in escape to her room. She tries on, and, models some of her other purchases. She looks of the flowers amongst the towns people. She puts on display, some fresh cuts that she purchased earlier that day. They dance in the vase, and, fresh water. She then, in fresh gear, descends into the lobby to speak with the clerk at the front desk. "What can I do for you Madame?" Coyly asks the clerk. "He's friendly enough." She thinks. As she decides to speak, sizing him up, she notices, as he busies himself to her attention, that he, too wear the crested charm. As she hears the chime, Cheri flashes back in thought to the airport, to Antoine, we recall the man at shore, now him. "Excuse me Madame?" He chimes again, in attempt to prove himself worthy of service. "Oui, Monsure." She starts in, as she cradles, and, shapes herself to naturality. Aheming, and, all. "Have I received any messages?" "Not any to date." They play. Back, and, forth. In, and, out. Up, and, down. Round, and, round they dance in verbal rhythms. "Well, thank you, anyway." She chimes back, confident that she's free for the evening. Remembering her pocketbook, she heads for the elevator, ascends again, and, heads for her penthouse door. She grabs her purse, gives her flowers a spin, and, heads out into the evening. Upon closing the door, the television, which has been on since her entrance, reports of the body that washed ashore earlier today. The headline reminds us of what Cheri might be in for. Was she ready for Antoine, his life, his habits, his adventure for energy? La Resistance would prove to be!

Atonement...

Enter, the Parisian square on this city night. Its festive atmosphere. Cheri makes her way through the night, taking in the Parisian air. Enchanted, she remembers herself, and, begins to inquire about to the locals about La Resistance.

"Pardone' moi. Auelle es La Resistance?" She requests of citizen after citizen. "Pardone' moi?" Form an ear's shot away, Dante' "Village" Dunn overhears. Now, he's a shady-type, not quite dark, an unbenounced to her he's Antoine's right-hand Man. Not the type to be assisting local travelers. In fact, he's not the type to be assisting anyone, but, himself at all. However, being that it's exactly where he's going, and, she is attractive, it does peak his attention. "What the hey." He follows a bit, observing her, then catching up to her, taps her on the shoulder. "Pardon me. Did you say La Resistance?" He lightly demands of her. "Yes, yes I did. You know of it?" She stutters, spinning around, half startled. Looking her over with a combination of intrigue, and, cynicism, he snickers out the invite, "Come with me, I'll show you."

"Lovely evening." She starts in right away, as they walk a short distance, and into an alleyway. "Yes it is." He comforts, as he leads her, sensing something curious. She seemed to bring out the provider in him, as he found himself exhibiting his escort round, and, about a care for her. Small talk was not his thing, yet, he found himself not minding. Measuring her response, and, approval, if even mildly. He sort of shrugs, and, shivers it off, continuing. "How did you fmd this place?" He lightly interrogates. "I was invited." She responds in badge, suddenly, surprisingly concerned with her questioned eligibility. "You?" She returns. "I'm a member."

It's stated so firmly, she begins to wonder about her position here. Perhaps she shouldn't have followed the stranger to this unknown place. Non of the convenient locals seemed to know about it. And, at night what was she thinking. Earlier, Antoine's invitation made it sound so at ease, so jovial, so innocent. Only now did it have a twinge of danger, did she second guess herself. Then, her slightly overdeveloped confidence kicked in. She's never taken to flight before, why should she start now? Besides, Antoine was just a breath's call away. Safety was around the bend. She just new that he would swerve in, and, save her from this flush of sudden insecurity. She just knew it. Cheri follows through, and, decides to proceed.

"A member, that's nice." She states, as they continue on to a non-descript, back door. Village knocks the "special knock," and, a window slides open. Roger, who's overseeing the door, gives Village a command in French. Village eyes the man. He doesn't like the command, but, Roger gives it again, this time Village complies. Reluctantly, where this was once a recreational humor, but, because of Cheri's presence, he hesitates to do a silly song, and, dance, rapid pace, and in French, that he fmishes quickly. Roger is amused, Village is approved, and, then the attention lies on Cheri. "Et Elle?" Roger demands. Village, returned to his bravado, finds the need to clue Cheri in. "You have to state your name, and, who you're here to see." Now, he's really interested, as the mystery comes to fruition, And, all eyes are now on her, and, her trial of admission. "My name is Cheri. I was invited by Antoine." She delivers. "Really?" Roger, and, Antoine exchange a glance. Impressed, and, in hands off mode, the red carpet rolls out. "Entrée. Roger obliges, and they do.

As, Roger closes the door, Cheri hears the same, charmed tinlding.

Who's Who?

They enter into an underground club in lull swing. Cheri's inventory of memories is slowed in motion: man at the airport (ring), Antoine (ring), Village (ring), and, now roger, who whispers pointedly at Village as he passes. "Where is your crest?" Village, with an intent to be oblivious, as he does not like to be checked on, moves to catch up with Cheri. "Just get the door." He coughs back, taking Cheri by the hand. "Come with me." Roger eyes him, transferring the cough, he barks out a command to the other doorman, "Get the door!" He does, and, the alleyway rests once again.

La Resistance! Electric, futuristic, alive. The popular gathering place, and, set free location. A cultural enthusiasts dream. La Resistance! Village leads Cheri through the crowd, as one of its featured group performs. He likes the attention. She likes the energy. He enjoys this moment, before having to turn his, well, Antoine's find over to himself. He surrenders his last words, "This way. I will introduce you to the owner."

They ascend a stair case, scale a hall, and, usher into a private room, as he leads her to a man, clearly the life of the party, entertaining an intimate group of people. Village gets his attention, and, directs it to Cheri. He is pleasantly surprised, and, takes her in. "Well, if it isn't the still beauty." Antoine receives, covering his amazement. He expects his word to be followed, yet, somehow, he wanted to be surprised by her. "You're sneaking up on me now." Cheri, covering her thrill, as she's just been flushed with the excitement within the familiarity of his voice. "If it works." She offers. "I hope so." He closes, enjoying the touché. Cheri, not having given herself away, feels him out. There is some tension, she cuts through. "So, this is you?" She melodies. "Along with my other two selves. Village," whom he grabs in an ambre, covering his delight in machismo, "Who is my pulse on the real life in Paris. And, Roger," he refers to the door, "career criminal, and, long time friend. Me?" He spies a featured piece of art he'd like to introduce her to, while she takes all of this in. "Well, this," he unravels, "this is me." He gestures to Village, who brings her to Antoine, who introduces her to the work. "If this is anything less than sensational, I'm taking you home, eh?" He gests, pulling his men into the humor. Cheri, refusing to reveal her hand, immediately moves to the piece to feel it out. She successfully arrives, and, takes in the work. She can only get the frame in, yet, manages, "It's lovely. You're right, I like it! Beyond what I could imagine. Amazing!"

While she is busy there, Village whispers something in Antoine's ear. Antoine nods to confirm, and, moves to retrieve Cheri. "Come with me, where I can better take you in." They go out the door, down the stairs, through the crowd, to the back door, near Roger, where they exit. Roger smirks, as he secures the door.

They spill out into the narrow by-pass. Free from all audible competition, where Cheri feels more at ease. She likes this playing hooky with Antoine. It makes the small alleyway liberating. Knowing her secret, Cheri finds her nerve. "So, this establishment, is it new?" She begins. "A couple of years now." Antoine admits. "It's so frill, so well thought out. I'm impressed." She discloses. Antoine, on a flush, decides to play his card, and distract. "Are you hungry? Let's go !" Playing commander, they make their way into the night.

Food for Thought!

Under the canopy of night, is provided the perfect back drop for the two of them, ambianced by street musicians, and free form performers, enjoying a midnight meal.

"Now, this reminds me of home." Cheri unwinds, brought to life by the undying allure of the enchantment that is called for on a "first." He seems to have gotten her flattered, and, cooed, but not overcome. "And that is?" He inquires, trying not to be thrown by her fresh innocence. They've clearly impressed one another enough to have made an impact on the other's time, and, are enjoying one another quite well. "New York. Business capitol of the world." She begins in again, taping into just enough to keep his casual attention. "Its earned the reputation of being the second, largest metropolitan on the globe." She finishes, and, for some strange reason, it is dine without thinking anything upon anything of her life there at all. "What do you do there?" He prods. "I play symphonic, concert piano." She matches. "Only classical?" Antoine counters. "I improvise a little. I've never really strayed far from classical composition." Chcri completes. "That will change." He thinks out loud. A bold subtext. She sees, and, raises him. "Really?" "*Yes,*." He demands, and, immediately he wants this so. "Come."

Taking her by the hand, he leads her t o an open portion of floor, and, proceeds to lead her in dance. Their rhythm is off beat at first. "Don't fight me, Just follow." He remarks, as he continues to guide her through his sway, and, step. They dance on. A little better. Still not fluid. Cheri buckles with snicker. "I'm sony, I swear I can dance. I can't explain." "No need to explain. You're just not ready to let me lead you yet. It's okay. It's good. I like it." Cheri takes in this moment, Antoine does as well. Someone not finding fault with her. "You're peculiar. I like you." She finally confesses. "The same." He agrees. "You know, aside from my own business, I followed you from the flower Shoppe. There was just something so beautiful about you in the day. I didn't want to stop watching you." Cheri, definitely affected, does finally blush. Then, in time, and, in the moment, he kisses her. It is sweet, tender, timeless. Antoine, fmally pulls away, dazzled. He finally forms the words, "Delicious. Much better, I will show you many things." As they dance on, he now spins her around.

The stars, they twinkle a bit.

Hotel Nicole

They have dined, scaled the sights, and, now Antoine has properly seen her home. "Well, here we are. I have truly enjoyed you. You couldn't have arrived at a better time." "Why, thank you, Antoine. You really do know how to have a good time in this city. I too have enjoyed." He kisses her hand, and, presents a rose. "To good times." Placing it in her hand, he inquires, "Will I see you again?" "I imagine, anything is possible here, right?" They kiss. "Bien?" "Bien.. . soft!"

With that, they part. As she is wituess of his departure, she feels the coast come clear. She then, walks ahead a ways, and, across the street to her true logging. A classic game of hide, and, seek. After all, a girl's got a right to her secrets. And, she didn't want the danger she felt earlier that evening. "Here's to thinking on your feet." She pronounces, as she enters into the revolving doors, and, thinks, "I followed you.' Ha! Indeed." Unseen by her, Antoine has witnessed the entire transaction, and, sights, "I see you! I do see you! Ha!" As he carries on, and, into the night.

Cheri's already been through the elevator, has breezed into her Penthouse, and, turned on the news, her eyes on the city, as she likes to keep on top of all that she couldn't otherwise see.

As Cheri takes in her lingual brush up, we turn to Robert, Cheri's Father, is in his legal offices, discussing the details of a case en route to his corner/bay. On the way, he catches sight of the Parisian exclusive from one of the common rooms. Invested, he enters the room, and, listens in on the breaking story.

"Breaking news. This is the latest in these murders. Police believe it to be connecter to some notorious, underground activity in the state of France. They alert citizens of the need for care, and, to be on the watch.

In other news..." The castor fades out, as Cheri's Father bolts out in Paternal overdrive, abruptly putting the breaks on his legal convo. "Yea, Jim. I'm gonna have to get back to you after lunch. Sounds good. Right." Immediately, he hangs up, and, dials for Cheri, whom he has to degree through her mother. Hoping none of this has reached her. While dialing for Mona, he brushes up against some of his colleagues on the way into his office. "Excuse me gentlemen." appropriates, arriving at his office, and, B-lining it to his desk. Finally, he gets Mona on the line. "Yes, Mona. Listen, I need to speak with Cheri." Mona, who is at Gelson's, is also buzzing with the heightened energy of city-wide preoccupation. "Really, well, I'm out, Robert. I don't have those details on me." Mona, knowing Robert's temperament, braces for the fight, remaining poised throughout her shopping. "You don't know?" He snorts. "You always did let the wind carry those girls." "Robert, don't you know Cheri? She has the flight, and, the hotel, but, no room. Or, The room, and, the hotel, but, not the city. Or, the city but not the number. The child is just that way. She just doesn't fmd the need to be thorough. Perhaps you can talk it into her this time." She gests. "What's going on? What's the fuss?" "Woman, I wouldn't trust you with me right hand attached to my body. Why I do it with my girls is beyond me. What's the hotel, at least?" "Robert, you've reached me on my mobile. It's at home. You owe Dana a call anyway. I know she has it. What's the emergency?" "Do you watch television anymore in your world? Don't you know they are killing people all over Paris?"

There is a pause over the phone, as reality brings Mona to her place. "Yes, Mona! Murders! Our daughter could be right in the middle of it!" Mona, now awake to the severity of this unexpected happenstance, gasps, and, eclipses her gaping mouth. "Oh, Robert. I didn't know." "No kidding." He garbles, sighing. "If you don't mind, I have to see about the safety of our child." "Good, when you fmd out, let me know." Why don't you call Dana." He Frustrates. "Touché." Mona concedes. Robert, absolutely on his wit's end. "Good-bye."

Two to Tango...

Eckertstein & Son. We are **with Robert as he makes** his call to Dana.

Dana is in dance rehearsal. She is lovely. Though she misses the call, she makes the note on step. To the finish! All present clap, as she prances into the wing. Comrades greet her. "Your phone, again." "Yea, can you put that thing on silent? It throws the count. And, you don't nearly pay enough." "Sure, sure." Dana convinces. "It's probably my work. Thanks." "No problem. You look good out there. Otherwise I would tell you to keep your day job." "You still auditioning for that company?" "Yea, you can't pull that off dancing this stuff. Where do you take again?" "Stratovarian: The Red Shoe." Dana announces. "Oooh....!" They all tease. "You know I wish you the best, right? Next time your phone rings, I'm charging you though." They laugh. "Thanks, guys. See you." She waves them good-bye, gathers her things, signs off with the instructor, and, a few more dancers, makes her way into the corridor, and, checks her phone. "Dad?"

An old anxiety hits her. Like an iron fist. She, and, her father have never really seen eye to eye. Cheri, on the other hand has always had her father's favor. "Please don't let this be about my sister." She grieves. She dials the number, awaiting his answer. Striking gold, she finally speaks. "Dad?"

"Dana, yes. Listen, I hate to be curt, honnie, but, what is your sister's travel information?" She sighs. "I knew it. And, how are you?" "I'm fine, honnie. Listen, can you hurry? This is important." "Yes, Dad, my proposal is going just fine. Yes, Dad, With the best of efforts, I should win this campaign." She is pointed, adamant, and, insistent. Robert, knowing, "Dana, not now." "Is she in trouble, again?" "I hope not, I've got to confirm. Can you at all put some speed to this?" He worries. "Alright, let me get it, it's in my phone. Do you mind?" She sets down her things, and, retrieves the information from his mobile. "No, I don't. You know, you're certainly smarter than your mother. Just lead-foot it baby." "She's at Hotel Nicole." Hurriedly, Robert writes the remaining information down on a legal pad. "Thanks, dear. I gotta go." He finalizes, abruptly clicking off. For, he' s got to go! Dana is amiss.

The empty hail echoes with her fmal words. "I love you too."

She gathers up her things, and, continues down the corridor.

Nick of Time!

Pick up on Cheri breezing in, and picking up on the news report about the earlier death. "Oh, my God!" She quickly, turns off the T.V., and opts for some lit candles, instead. The phone rings. She answers. "Hello?" She listens. "Dad? How did you get this number?" She continues to listen, and respond, fill of complaint. "Maaaaaaan!" She's hating life right now! She shuffles, two-steps, and, double times to his paternal interrogation. "No, Dad.. .1 didn't.. .1 just.. .Yes, dad. I saw the news report, and I'm fme. Everything's fine!" The phone beeps. "One moment, father..." She clicks over. "Hello?" She listens. "MARCUS??? How did you??? MOTHER!!!" As her cry reverberates in echo.

Cheri couldn't wait to take a bath after that one. For she had been completely impenetrated. She had been uncovered, discovered, and, all around Benedict Arnold! Why did her confident resources have to give her up? She was frustrated, at odds, and, in need of some emergency R&R! So, she took it, and, took it she did!

We hear the sound of splashing water. We see bath water spilling onto the floor. Back to Cheri. "Oh, no! The bath! Look, Marcus.. .1 don't know why you're calling, but.. .DON'T!" With that, she hangs up the phone, and, darts to the tub, turning the nozzle to off. The phone rings again (Dad on hold). She darts back to the phone. "Dad! It's my bath... I will.. .gotta go! Bye!" As she darts back to the bathtub.

Cheri has safely squared away everything with her mother. It was her Dad's ignorance, and, her lack of communication with him that led to Marcus' ultimate reveal of her whereabouts, unfortunate for her. She soothes all of that with a conversation with the safest presence on earth, her mother.

Cheri on the phone with her mother, "I'm fine, Mom. I'm blind, but, I'm not helpless. What's going on with Dana?" Mona, is in her car, driving amongst the traffic, again. "Honnie, you know your sister is sensitive." Cheri, rolls her eyes, and, scoffs, "She's also a privileged, pain in the but!" Mona, caught off guard, honks her horn, shouting something in mid-traffic New Yorker, keeping perfect timing with Cheri. "Okay, let's watch what you say about your sister, shall we? It reflects upon you. I want PG conversation here. She's just as concerned as we all are about you." 'Well, what she say, if anything?" "That you need to go to church! Ha!" As Mona has gotten a good one in. "Ha! What!!!" "Yes, she did. She really did say that!" Mona scores. "Ha! No she didn't 'I need Jesus' me! Ha!" They laugh. "Yes she did!" Mona gathers.

"Well, ha! Ha! Ha! I know she has her nose in my business then. Thanks, ma! What she say about the split?" "Well, she agrees with your father, and, I. That you need to revamp, and, invest in those precious 8-years." "No!... I'm not being bull nosed here! You know I need to clear my head of that." Yes, honnie. But, refresh that stock. Don't sell it. For the sake of your heart." Not what Cheri wants to hear at all. In fact, she's down right indignant. "Gotta go!"

As she clicks off, and, thinks a bit. Cheri, emerges, damp from the water. Dances a few more steps to the bed, where she collapses, deep in thought, and, purrs off to sleep.

Le Matain!

Cheri, is so taxed, that she has remained in the same position throughout the night. She is awakened by a knock on the door. In her Penthouse hallway, we see the room service waiter, who calls out. "Room service." Cheri slumbers over to the door, opens it, and, lets in the server, who sets up her morning breakfast. "Your breakfast, Madame." "Right over there, thank you." She charges.

She signs the receipt, and, goes to freshen up. He concludes set up on the terrace, and, exits her room. She crosses out to dine, brought to life, as she bathes in the morning sun. Indulging in the sights, and, sounds of the Parisian morning, she becomes acclimated to France once again. Taking in the sights with her, we also take in an invader, Marcus! Exiting his taxi, to enter the lobby!

Hotel Nicole, lobby, morning. An exhausted Marcus makes his way to the front desk for check in. "Hi. Marcus Erickson." The receptionist looks onto the computer. "Oui, Monsieur. I'll need your credit card for incidentals." He's got it ready for her. As she takes it. "Oui, Monsieur. There is much t do along the village way, right outside. Many shoppes, and thing of that nature. The Concierge can provide more details, if you like." "Thank you." He thinks a beat, then, "Excuse me, is there any information you could give me on a Cheri Coles? A guest here at your hotel." "Monsieur, We cannot disclose the confidential to anyone." "Well, if you should find anything of interest to me   He hands her a thousand dollar bill. "Oui, Monsieur." The receptionist accept it very discreetly.

"Thank you, again." He clues, as he crosses to the front doors.

Marcus makes his way with a defmitive awkwardness through the crowd of shop sport. Knocked, and, bumped by the crowd, he progressively builds with irritation. Weary from hours of travel, he makes his way sure. The sure fight of one, very tired man. He manages into a clothing store, and, proceeds to cross over to the tailored wears, when a store clerk intercepts. "May I assist you, Monsieur?" He offers. "Yes, I'd like something of your highest quality, finely tailored." "Hinmm   He peers over to his coworker. Marcus, just surfaces with irritation, which he lets out in a sigh. "Look, my luggage got lost by the airlines. I need to see your latest line." Oui, Monsieur. I do apologize. Please, come." With New York alive in hhn, he pointedly blows off some excess steam. "Thank you.. .Merci to you too."

After purchasing his wears, the only other, logical thing to do was to accessorize them. So, conveniently he went about doing that. Shoppe, after shoppe, he examined, and, purchased, examined, and, purchased, examined, and, purchased until new, and, improved, replacement wardrobe, ensemble, and, all was complete. With that to his credit, he, finally, is able to embrace the city.

In need of refreshment (a shower, some good food, and, some much needed rest), and, the logging of his things, Marcus heads for the hotel, when suddenly, he is started to attention, recollecting a pressing piece of business. "Oh, God! The Intium Sock!" He goes to access his phone. No service. Marcus has reached the pinnacle of his frustration, and, begins to take it out on his phone. Then, eureka! An alternative!

"My room phone!" In need to keep on top, he high tales it into the hotel lobby, and up the elevator.

Code White!

Marcus bursts through the door, dives for the phone, and, dials. The call comes up a recording. Marcus is about to have an aneurysm. "Doggon international codes!" He scrambles for the hotel's international sheet, and, dials the number again. This time he gets the receptionist, Donna. "Bernstein &Lindenplatt." "Yea, Donna, this is Erickson, put me through to Bernstein." "Sure thing. Please hold." As he holds, he riffles through every step. All that needs to be said, and, done. Then, "This is Jacob." "Hey, Jay. You're going on that Intium Stock today, right?" "Good." Why? What's up? Where are you?" "I'm in Paris." A male moment, then, "Wow...1 wish you the best, Marcus." "Thanks." He hangs up the phone, and picks up an article that has caught his attention.

The headline reads: "Suspected 'Black Market' Under Investigation for Recent Homicides."

The last thing he needed to see. He falls onto the bed, and, takes a moment to collect himself. He then, stands to his feet, and, begins to unpack. Determined to fmd Cheri. First, he must get presentable.

Marcus turns on shower, orders room service, dismantles, robes up, and, begins his transform. While in the shower, a knock at the door interrupts his heaven. It's room service. The waitress politely makes herself known. Marcus gets out, signs the receipt, and, sits down to indulge, as she exit's the room. He fmishes his meal to satisfaction, and, stretches out across his bed. As he stares contemplatively at the ceiling, and, slowly surrenders to sleep, h~ thinks, gets an idea.

Paris city streets. Marcus is definitely on the hunt for Cheri. Looking through the crowd of on goers. Seeing almost, but, no cigar replicas of Cheri. Checking in with front desk to retrieve any, and, all messages. Finally,

Marcus is dining at a café, rehearsing what he is to say to Cheri. He jots down thoughts on note pad. "I don't understand. I've done everything you wanted me to do. Now I need you to do something for me." He crumples paper. "I've done well as an attorney, like you wished, just like your father. Why cant you see that the life I built is best for us?" Crumples paper. Thinks a beat, then, "You're not going for any of this are you?" Writes, "How do I reach you? Where are you? What are you doing? What are you trying to prove?"

Satisfied with his outline, Marcus continues, though disturbed to plan out his saving of Cheri from herself Certain that she was on some self-retrieving course. We leave him there, as he carries on his meal.

"Dor Me Vous?"

The scene was lovely that day. The field, plush. The stream, clear. The trees in willow. Though Cheri cannot see, she is in tune, and, has set the scene for a perfect outing. Lying out, and, organizing a light meal for two.

Antoine, being given specific instruction on direction, knows the location well. Surprisingly, it's where he go to do most of his thinking. He arrives well, walking up, and, spotting her there. He miles, "Hello, you." She looks up, smiles, and, waves him over. How picture perfect! The two of them on their first outing. Tis every bit of perfect. He, and, her, with no one else around, but, the stream, and, the landscape, and, the charming willows.

Antoine lays on a blanket, as Chcri plays the familiar tune "Aloetta" on a portable keyboard. There, the lunch spread is complete with sparkling champagne. She sings the song, as Antoine decides to introduce her to its meaning. Playfully kissing each pronouncement. They indulge, and, dine under the shade of a nearby tree.

"Do you know the meaning of that song?" Antoine introduces. "Well, mostly." Cheri duets. "I learned it in grade school. So long ago." Antoine, up for the opportunity to instruct, directs her to continue her play while he organized his. "Let me show you." He says, gathering some pillared candles from the basket. "What are you doing?" Cheri is curious. "If you don't mind, I'm going to use some of theses candles here." He busies. "I was going to use those for later, Antoine." "Well, I'm going to show you now." He insists. "Lay down, facing skyward, and, allow me to do the rest." He instructs. "Sing." She does, softly. "Aloetta, gentil Aloetta. Aloetta, Je te plus me res." "Okay, now stop." He orchestrates, placing a candle by her head, and, lighting it. "Now, go" She does. "Je te plus me res la tet." "Stop." He delicately kisses her forehead, then explains. "You see, this song is about a little bird, who signs so sweet that you want to eat it up. And, you do. Piece by piece, and, in order." He confesses. Only, I'm going to kiss you. Proceed." She does, and, so does he. She pronounces the course of feast, and, he reward her. First her arm, then her leg. They both smile, giggling, as they both know what's next. Cheri sings, "Je te plus me res Ia plume." He kisses her heart She sputters with laughter. "This has been nice." She concedes. "Not over yet, come." He takes her by the hand, rising to his feet, inviting her to join him.

They dance, swaying under the wil low within the frame of her candle lit body.

Atone...

Antoine, and, Cheri are now by the lake. Antoine lies on his back. Cheri postures herself at his side. With everything that has been going on, Antoine is at peace in his leisure. They both enjoy the quiet, as they chat.

"So, you clever girl, how could you have had any clue as to what I would like?" "You liked?" "Yes." "I guess I'm just good at what I do." They enjoy. "Nice to be appreciated." You know what else T'd appreciate, if you'd take your elbow out of my side, that really hurts." "oh." They laugh, they share, he's relieved. "You know, in come countries, that custom is probably the highest of compliments. I think I'll travel there, next." Oh, really, and, where is this you would go?" Antoine requires. Oh," she teases. "Somewhere free. Somewhere I can fight against oppressive expression, and, effect the slightest change amongst those who would live that way. How would you know? This is who I have come to be." "Paris isn't free for you? Come, let me show you. I have fooled you I think."

He rises to help her gather her things, blowing out candles, bottling the champagne, and, leading her along the initial path through which he entered, he escorts her right to his motorcycle. Cheri, not at all intimidated, is surprised by his generous gesture, and, finds herself intrigued by its form. "What is this? She investigates. "My, very large bicyclette. Now, come." "Night clubs, motorcycles. You're just full of surprises aren't you? Very interesting, though, I'll have to admit." "Don't give me so much credit yet." He blushes. "Let's go.

Secretive by nature, it was unlike Antoine to be so fluid with his character. Generally, serious, isolate, mysterious even, Antoine wondered at this, new, liberation of what he held so dear. A sport for adventure, he allowed affect to play, pondering, in motion, what this meant for him. How did he, so naturally, care so well about someone he had just relatively met? Premature for him, sure, but, he liked her, and, was driven to go with it. As he does, he has in mind to show her the greater love for Paris, detecting the unusually strong allure to keep her there with him. He enthuses, as he invites her, willingly, to his surprise into one of his many layers.

While Antoine sets this up, his men move in for business. A remote, off the path, abandoned warehouse sets the scene for such an exchange. Outside of this, industrial, structure nondescript men move in at a pace that defines the line of activity. Above the law.

They've been waiting to make this trade for months, now, and, Antoine has been in expectation of new product. Good thing for them, they had it. Though working the darker areas of commodity, it was not narcotics that Antoine was trading, but art. restricted, and, black listed, Antoine became heir to an entire world of exotic wares, affording him an entire, global, network in a class all its own. Demand, high, supply, plenty., as the wealth of the world turned to him for their highly prized adornments. He neither depended on it, nor, had to do it, but, he was good at it, so he engaged. If conquer the world through this affluent avenue was what was available to him, then conquer the world was what he was going to do. Simple.

At this very moment, Antoine is having the time of his life. With Cheri. They tour the city, he explains on the way to the genesis of Antoine. One, of his favorite places. La Lourvre. Arriving, they free themselves of the bike, as he begins to remark to her about it.

This, one of the earliest, and, most prized of the houses of art boasts pieces that boast each of a conquest. The reign of a king. From the classic, to the Renaissance, to the romantic, this very building is an innovation to time itself. "I see, "Cheri remarks, "and, how do you find your peace here?" "Here is where I remind myself to be great, that is all. There is more." He assures. "Come." They, hand-in-hand, walk into this world.

Meanwhile, The men take part to their meeting. Opposing team in Place, serious business, we never, really, see their faces, as they mean what they presume. Secret is kept. This flag of transaction is prime, as Antoine sees this as the ultimate opportunity to build, and, set his empire.

In their own world, Cheri, and, Antoine take a ride on a tram. To a destination known only by him. Silent with their plays of affection, they wituess, as life goes by, and, become a partner to:

A man, engrossed with his daily newspaper; a middle-aged woman, sitting with her of age son, knitting; a business, no-nonsense type, complete with briefcase, and, trench coat; A young woman that climbs on board with her little dog, little shoes, and, hurt feet; fmally, an older woman, devout in her faith, sits with the sanctity of her rosary beads.

They exult in the language of their quiet. Steeling a kiss here, a snuggle there, and, high on life, they pronounce their silent romance into the quiet sky. Hoping, above all, that their, playful, infatuation wins the day.

Back to the exchange, exchange is made. Large packages of goods for briefcases. A successfhl transaction. The men line up, as this shipment spells the bottom line. All accounts closed, the house wins the day.

Meantime, at the site of E'glise St-Germain l'Auxerrois, the site of Antoine's sanctuary, they reach their destination, and, then, disembark. Antoine confesses, "This, is, finally, where I fmd my peace. While they're at this bigger than life, Gothic church, Antoine wants to confess some new feelings for her. Complete with stained glass, and, cathedral ceilings, Cheri, secretly sings from her heart, "So far, I've only found mine through music. This should prove to be amazing." "Not yet." Antoine pronounces.

Meanwhile, Antoine's men, and, those present for the deed done, make their way to the vehicles that have been in wait. Having arrived at this sight of, final, destination, they shake hands, pile in, each satisfied with their portion, and, drive off. Again, as Antoine has wanted, and, as Antoine has expected, Antoine receives. Mission accomplished.

The Biffel Tower, in all its high, standing glory is impressive to take in. Antoine, enthralled by the role the guiding expert, makes full advantage of the wealth of his technical, facts, and, figures regarding the ins, and, outs of Europe's most famously, prized structures. As he begins to explain: "This, the great, Eiffel Tower, is the largest, and, most celebrated configurations in all of France. "Yes, this I understand. I have heard so much about it." She flatly states, amid her attempt to, truly, encompass this all too, known framework of high majesty. "You seem unimpressed." He examines. "Iwouldn't say, 'unimpressed'. It'sjust that 'La Lourvre' seemed more 'you.' The kings, the greatness." She reviews. "You think so?" He inverts. "Yes, yes, I most certainly do. Now, tell me, how does this capture you?"

"It's 107 feet high," he exacts, "lays claim to all, 10,000 tons of it's total mass weight. It's already a world monument, and, can boast to bringing the world together. Last, but not least, It is the, youngest piece of art here. Good enough?" "Interesting. Very interesting." She confesses. "I'll say." He owns. Then, grabbing her by the hand, he proceeds. "Come."

In the alleyway of La Resistance, there is an aggressive movement. Antoine's men, nondescript, get out of, and, unload the cars. There is a hurried rush, as orders are barked. "Move! Move!" The men order themselves, and, step up their activity. "Move it!"

Meantime. Versailles lays the format for Antoine's latest, and, concluding reveal. Cheri, and, Antoine walk, and, talk. "We're in the Versailles, now. And, this," he offers in presentation, "is the 'Hall of Mirrors.' It's where

I come to find myself, always. I reconstruct" "This, definitely registers, impressive. Outstanding. You." "Exactly. I think this is all for today. Let's go." Antoine, and, Cheri seemed to bond, developing commonalities, held close to heart, save, the occasion to affect. They enjoyed each other, genuinely. Harboring no apology to the surrounding critique, and, or, infiltration. Wishing, storing their affections into the rays of sun. The future, a whisper of promise. They were in love. But, dared not quote. Wishing on stars, and, holding time in bottles was now in season, and, in fashion. They would bid. The hope for love pulsated throughout each, new scene. The allure to conjoin, restrained. Two sparks, contracted to passion. Refrained by the mold.

En report to the evening, t' is apparent that Cheri faces, and, will become directly confronted with that, all time, and, chronically involved decision, of pay, or, play. Knowing her hour glass was fast running out, Cheri, felt the heat, but wasn't about to sweat, as Antoine delivered her safely, and, on time to her come' cozy.

On location, at her hotel, Cheri strolls in, past the lounge, just missing Marcus. They do not see each other.

Marcus, who has revered Cheri, for the greater portion of his obstructed, tumultuous, and, lackluster life, has foiled himself in the looseness of his cruelty. Cheri has been the foundation, and, the motive behind the celebration in his life for the major part **of eight years.** When he had her, when she was his, he relished her, built his entire, professional world from her inspiration, constructed the whole of his image par her expression, but, he didn't love her. And, it showed.

Sure, he could buy the lion's share of tangible affects in symbol of his affections. Amass enough wealth to support a life of high style, and, coveted luxury. Recite enough amorous affirmations to meet the needs of the spines of several romance columns. But, did he love her? Latest forecast revealed desolate reports. There was the championing that was wanting, his sincerity that rated low, and, the attention to the olithic details that were all together missing. These breaks in the pattern left gaping holes, razed cultures, and, teetering confidences that had given fray to the wind long ago. His, listless, attempt to recover what was lost to the realm of time, and, fallen efforts would, now, fall to discriminate ears, and, cynical heart..

He holds to his last, remaining tie-line. Her father. Marcus bluffs his way through the conversation, siphoning swatches of information he passes off as good advice. Loading his symposium with pardons, and, excuses in the all out effort to win her back from the allure of Paris, from the hysterical, power play of the displays of her independence, from the humbling truth regarding his villainous arrogance. Marcus, is on the outs.

Treading thin ice, he carefully gives camouflage to all he's about to say. She's been his property for so long he fmds himself having to taper his overgrown sense of entitlement, and, indignance. More a possession than a companion, Cheri fled so that she could develop that which she could salvage from the clearing of the tempest of Marcus' poor skill in relationship. It served her right to exercise her option to free herself into bloom of her own choices. Her own, set individualism. Her own intuatives, and, inner motive. Marcus, had a fight ahead of him, and, Cheri was the item.

Undefeated, and, contented with her newly claimed liberties, Cheri would not go into this night quietly. Marcus, was in for the trial of his life. Court, judge, and, hammer. Gavel, burden, and, proof. He'd have to dance ten-thousand swords before she'd win away the slightest give. Marcus would have to bend.

This being clear, he codes in to every filament available. Every advantage sighted.

"Yes, I'm here. No, I've not found her. I'm positioned well, so I can succeed in my trappings. She' probably out, somewhere, feeding her face, if not shopping." He Gapharphs. "Never be afraid to admit when you're wrong, Marcus. Now would be the time to divulge that you don't know heads, or, tails when it comes to my daughter." He invises. "Sir, when it comes to your daughter, and, I, I take the high road, because I have to answer to you." "And, now...?" Robert assuages. "Sir, I've come into my own. I simply want Cheri to catch up." "Well, son, that game sounds about as good for Cheri, as my good, right foot." Robert tiffs. Marcus rolls his eyes, and, clears his throat. "Watch it now. What I'm saying is this: you know that my daughter is special. One in a million. If you were true to your heart, you'd have her. Now, you've got to make up on a probated plate. And, with that attitude. As you find the opportunity, seize it. Let's hope you'll find what to say." "I appreciate that, Mr. Coles." Marcus indicts. "Listen," Robert imports, "go to court. Handle your affairs. You're going to need the advantage. She caught you by surprise, now, catch her. Now, I've got to handle something." He rises. "Don't let her railroad you, 'cause she will. Let's hope for your best effort."

Getting off the phone was refreshing. Then, an uneasiness set in. What would he use to win her? Where was her mind? And, in the grand, scale of things, where would this put them, now? FTc reaches for the hotel pen, and, pad, and, begins to write. "Cheri,".

Toast Coast!

Cheri, combs through the day, committing noteworthy moments to memory, enveloped in her rose pedal, bath. With Marcus miles away from her world of gourmet patisseries, high fashion boutiques, and, expensive port locales, Cheri, can, now, ease into the budding enchantment of the new possible. The, tender, reveal, and, fresh aware of allure, authentic. With Antoine, the fondness captured became delicate veneers of attachment. Affect collages, dance, and, spin within spaces, untouched. This, charmed, undertaking of unveiled affections lay bare fond bloom within the measure of the season.

Images play to her mind, clear as morning light. Settled, and, unfiltered. As she profit's the frame by frame chimera of mental incarnation, Cheri, transfuses all known past to present life within the sentiment, and, data available to her rasp. Occupied in expression, she toils, in thoughtful pose, at the day's blend. Then, rising, she buffs into what will prove to be the night's bidding.

Over the river, and, through the woods, Marcus sits, stationed in the hotel lounge. Full effect of the lobby in full view. He nurses an early, evening cocktail. "Well, old boy," he pronounces, "now is the moment of truth. Let's put this one on glory." With that, solitary, toast, he determinedly takes down the, remaining, Jack Russell, and, vows, "Never again shall I force this hand, Cheri. Never again shall I force this hand."

Local news reports in segmented repose on trouble in the city. Apparently, the workings of the underground were hailing closer to the surface. They spoke of a body washed ashore. Of, suspected, illegal activity. Of the witness trauma amongst those committed to the sighting. Cheri, adorns her form amid taking this in. Against her alarm, she directs her awareness into the evening. Antoine was there, and, versus all danger he would guard. Her, young, hopes key up in relieved smile. She employs her evening scent, clips on remaining adornments, and, proceeds into the night's stir. What awaits her is the beginning of a world of rotating vice, and, iniquity. A world of legend, and, of secrecy. A world of relative truths, and, contrasting theories. In this world, Cheri, would meet the head of the serpent.

Coming off of the same news report, from the lounge, Marcus, immediately darts in thought to Cheri. He needs to find her. Now. He's pledged her safe return, and, this, new, detail was not going to make that any less successful. Checking his wrist watch, he begins to head upstairs, figuring the need to get a steak on the city. Where she would be. The places to which she would show up. This needed to begin sooner than later, but, first, he would check the front desk for any leads. As he directs himself to this hopeful sourjourn, he receives a call. Upon accept, it is the airlines. He learns that his luggage has been found, and, will be delivered to him in the morning. He politely thanks them, and, hangs up the phone.

Par his approach, Marcus, averts in thought once more to the news report regarding the, suspected, underground crime ring. Knowing Cheri, he hadn't much to worry about. For, she could handle herself, evaded most trouble, and, didn't need much looking after. Yet, held in balance, was the fact that this was a new city, with new people, and, new trouble on the lurk.

"Where are you, Cheri?" He asserts, in thought, knowing he, too, has got to barter with time. Then, upon recognition of the, earlier, friendly, face, he registers an expectancy of retrieval. "Any news?"

Cheri, a fresh, portrait of pure innocence, enters the hall, from her penthouse, and makes her way to the elevator. As always, she's running a little late. She had to call to make arrangements to get to La Resistance, for her escort was not presently available. "La soft, it will forgive me." She dictates. "Here we go."

Out of the elevator, she bounds. "Anything in, regarding my earlier request?" Marcus petitions. "Not as yet, Monsieur." She replies with a light, sympathetic curl of her lip. He offers another $100 bill. "Games not up 'till I get my fox." He affirms.

Cheri, unaware of Marcus' determined pursuit, slips right past the whole of them, and, into the night.

Shoutes, and, Ladders.

Cheri, walks, dances, and, feels her way through the crowd, to the bar, as, another, outstanding, band performs. "Martini, dry." She orders. End of song, she's on the move, again. Squeezing through the pulsing congestion to get to the stairwell. Where she is met by Village. "Mon, petite. Pleasure to see you." Cheri, blushes. He measures her, and, then, states the mention, "Come." He pulls her onto the floor, and, begins to dance, seeing if she's got anything that would amuse. He pulls her in close. "Sorry, I could not be there for you tonight. Glad you made it. Antoine will be happy." He assures. Cheri, smiles at the allure of it.

Antoine, Owner, head, and, ring-leader of it all, steps out upon the upper level to get a cat's eye view of all he's acquired, and, all that he will succeed. Getting wind of the news reports was a necessary evil, an unwelcomed interruption to affairs that be. The, otherwise, that he kept on the hush. Only thankful that, now, they could reorganize, and, discharge on levels that would prove undetected. With that, he could deal. The rest, he could do blindfold.

Mid taking in of his amassings, Antoine spots Village. Dancing with Cheri. Amused, he set's his position. The old "game" is on. Not since childhood, has a woman been so vested. Antoine has always enjoyed the sharp competition brought about by Village's charm, but this was one round he would not loose, one prize he would not forfeit over to Village, one dance he would win.

Song ends. Village, and, Cheri, both breathless. Cheri, not quite sure the meaning of the experience. Without warning, village grabs Cheri again. This time, leading her to the stairwell. "So, you came to my aid, after all." She jaunts. "My pleasure, always." He assures.

As he moves, to continue the ascent, he is stopped, and, comes face to face with Antoine, who measures the scene, carefully. Village, and, Antoine lock in knowing glance. "Here is the lady of the evening." Village concedes, gesturing passage to Antoine. "Mademoiselle." His last words, as, he skirts past Antoine, to carry out the celebration.

Cheri, is frozen, as, Antoine, has not left sight of her. Once the jubilee has passed into the passing atmosphere, he receives her under shielded spark. Receiving her again into his sight, he veils glisten. Cheri, is unsure how to respond. She makes motion for a distract. "Ahem." She clears her throat. "The powder room, on this level?" "Clever girl." His expression clicks, and, then aflirms, "Strait, this way." As he escorts his guest, par her request, he is, again, crossed by Village, to whom he snaps. Village freezes. He sees Cheri through. Then, turning his attention to village, once more, he addresses, "Next time, you turn her to me, and, I mean immediately."

Now, Village, who has advanced with Antoine all of his life, was the gaming sort that Antoine grew up, and, therefore could afford to have around. In his reality, loyalty was a commodity, rare, and, distinguished beyond the forbidden. He was a necessary novel, not an inexpendable.

"What's the matter, Antoine? Afraid I've got too much game for you?" Antoine, immediately, snaps in , locking sight to the N-th degree of this retinal problem. Question answered. Moving beyond, Antoine addresses, "Where's your crest?" There is a moment that plays forever. Village knows Antoine has spoken. The missing crest would have to be answered for. Village calculates in a panic never before expressed. He arrives, and, counters. "I've got it. We're ago."

Under Antoine's glare, Village shrinks to size. Half of him wishing to deck Antoine. Half of him wishing for Cheri's narrow escape. A minute more, and, he'd be all, but, uncovered, but he spots his salvation, Cheri, fresh, and, alive. He seizes the moment. "Shall I begin immediately?" He gestures to Cheri, who, intercedes, with timely appointmentation. "Gentlemen, shall we?"

A Nick in Time

A package arrives, Antoine is alerted. He barks some commands in French, the men get to moving, including Village. Satisfied, the unfinished business is in his favor, he transfers the attention, again, to Cheri, who embraces him with open face. "You made it back." He remarks, full of steam, thankful to have her near. "Yes, I did." She sparks back. "So, where are we going?"

Now, Antoine, amused by this, latest, fleur, has never allowed himself to be taken under charge. This, exception, is, somehow, proving a pleasant interference to his pattern of risky element. Whatever she wanted, and, for what ever she'd ask, he'd deliver.

A man of his word, he covers sentiment by presenting her with a map. A map of the world. "Here." He reprieves. "You chose well, this trip. How shall you select, again? Any where you want, anywhere, we'll go." Now, Cheri, isn't the fly by the seat type. Even this, change of life, excursion took, fme-combed, decision making, and, was thoroughly thought out, and, planned. So, to surprise her with this task, so, directly, involved with the unknown factor of his hush-hush affairs, started her senses a bit, causing the least bit of suspicion to prick her subconscious. "Ready?" ~efore she can properly calculate affairs to make up her mind, the man of action has called her to decision. "Come. Choose." He politely demands. "See," as he places one of her hands, to cover his eyes, and, the other, he molds to direct his forefmger, "all you have to do," he spins the globe, "Is tell me." She lets the globe spin, and, presses his fmger, until there is a clear, defined stop. The selection is China. He opens. "Very well. I like your touch. If it's the Orient you want, then to the Orient we go."

Both, press a relief of laugh, as the two merging worlds meld unwittingly, unchangeable. They are growing fond despite the warnings, despite the danger, despite the aire. A moment, the recognize each other in smile. He grasps for her remaining hand, pressing a kiss. She beams a bit. "So, what do you have planned for tonight?" He looks at her, as if to order the world. And, mean it. Decides to shave it down a bit, and, simply responds, "Everything. Come."

Street Life

They trot past street dancers to Antoine's car. Excited by her pleasantness, he spins, embraces, and, kisses her breathless. She recovers in gracious blush. "I'm glad you decided to join me." He exhales.

He opens the door, seats her in, secures himself, and, they're off.

As Antoine speeds along under the night sky, Cheri, exists within the most, freeing, sense of liberation. The wind, the ecclesiastical canopy, the engine rnsh. There is no resource to compare, no coordinates to its peak, no way she wants to stop. They measure each other in the ethereal silence. He's about to break her inhibitions open wide, and, both, are about to find out that she's ready.

Antoine picks up the speed of the car. Cheri, becomes the portrait of braced courage. Antoine looks over to see if now is the time. He measures, it is. So, he goes.. .fast.

Cheri, caught off guard, gasps, and, positions herself to embrace the unexpected. Antoine is amused. Cheri, holds on for dear life. For her, this personal evolution just took a turn into her wildest dreams. It's fly, or, die for her. Antoine, likes. Cheri, does not.

"Nowhere fast is soon approaching." She thinks. "Your pride is not going to hold through this. Please, say something." A long way form the familiar security of X, and, Y train stations. Though this is not what she had bargained for, she almost, stubbornly, refused to look back. She just couldn't stomach the long look, on her return home, with no, reported, fmesse, the, dull, conundrum of the well traveled, congested city. Yes, she wanted adventure, but, not at the expense of her better judgment. Excitement, not at the abandon of rnle, and, order. She'd put her life in the hands of a man who knew nothing of her delicate operative, nothing of the secret she held close. A man, who's actions she could neither expect, foresee, or predict. "What is this you have done?" She ftighted, inwardly, vowing never to allow her life this far out of control, again. A moment of hold, and, then the voice comes in, strongly. "Antoine, stop. Stop the car, now!" "You sure? Because I know what I'm doing." He eases. "That's beside the point, isn't it. I don't like this." She insists. "Hold on tight, and, trust me. Okay?"

Antoine, on a sure course, was, now, inwardly thrown. He could feel her discomfort ache in his teeth. He hadn't meant to alarm her. But, he did know what he wanted. And, he did know what he was doing. Short of putting her into frenzy, he had to know that this draw upon him could pull through. He was on the cill of major moves. And, wanted this bad. He had to know. Gear shift. He had to know.

Executive call. The, high-speed, pursuit builds momentum. Even, from within himself, he had to know this would conceive. Gear shift. Cheri, is on fringe. Would this man be the death of her? She held, still, simulating flight. Loving life, more than all of this jeopardy, she vowed to touch ground with a new sense of care.

The star chase crescendos in high styled 180. Gear shift. Antoine, simultaneously, grabs for Cheri, and, slams on the breaks. As they spin, Cheri, is in awe, and, planing at level of grace. Amidst the tempest, they lock eyes. Cheri, is forever changed. Antoine, forever thankful. They've merged, again. In the blend of life force, tenacity. A mutual respect, a loyalty, now, contracted between them. "He" becomes "her". And, "they" are forever conjoined.

In tears, highly upset, Cheri, explodes in fresh rage.

"Why, would you do that?" She bargains. "Why, would you not consider me in all your horseplay?" Antoine is taken aback. He responds very carefully. "Now, Cheri   "I told you I didn't like it!" She intercedes. "But, you just had to zoom, zoom. Didn't you?" "Cheri..." He contests. "Antoine, I don't agree. In fact, I strongly disagree! You hear me?" "Cheri, what I did is what I did. We survived. We made it! Don't you see that?" "Made what? Made the news? Made me mad? Made your day? What?" Cheri, at wit's peak. "Okay," Antoine breathes, "If we can't celebrate, then we're nowhere." "Celebrate? You come in, and, my world just about comes crashing down. My life is sacrificed to the wind, and, you're only remark is to celebrate? That's darling!" She screams. "Just darling." "You know, you are going to champion this with me, if it's all I can take. Now, what gives with you?" He shouts. "I'm blind." She confesses. "What?" He insists. "I'm blind you fool! Do you have any idea what that is like?" She squeezes her cry into a whisper.

"Blind? You mean, you can't see?" "Blind. You mean, you can't see?" She mocks. "No! I'm stupid for getting in this car with you! That's what I am!"

Antoine is dumbfounded. Looks at her with, new, wonder. "I   he manages. "I've worked very hard to achieve my independence," she cuts through, "my confidence. And, yet I nearly let you tear that down in one, joy ride. You must be crazy! I mean, Ijust saw my life flash.F" "See! I've cured you!" Antoine attempts amid nervous humor. "Don't you dare mock my state." She revs. "Don't you dare! Or, I'll tell you exactly what it is that I see!"

Antoine, takes a moment to decide whether, or, not to continue speaking. Then, "Please, allow my apology. I suppose I did push a little on the impress. I've been showing you all day. I wanted you to see that side of me too." "Ha!" She jests. "And, what? I'm supposed to give you a grand, "welcome, horn; hero?' Hmm?" She contests. "Well, I don't want to. You could really have hurt me back there."

Now, if there were ever a time to be received, again, within Cheri's, good, graces, this was it. "Cheri, you know," he moves to touch her hand.. She retrieves, in poise of her discovery. He continues. "Maybe, you don't. But I would never hurt you. I wanted to excite you for something special." "What is that ?" He dares, "My, recovery. That, great, kiss of spirit" "A kiss? Have, I, no, want, from, you, for, anything, more?" She revelates. He dares further, "Look. I want you to have." Cheri, fights for her right, force. Then, veils, to, blush, and, explosion of laughter. And, concedes. "I'm gonna tell you, the next time..." "Shh   He interrupts. "I really didn't mean to frighten you so. Perhaps, first, you can see me." He moves to touch. She softens. He takes her hand, and, warms to it softly. Upon receipt for continuance, he, gingerly, takes her hand, placing it upon his face. Her sensories are at once alerted. Finally, an image to embrace.

He's in awe, as he can feel her delicate search. Sense her own wonder. Drink in her pulse. He closes his eyes, "I apologize." He is breathless. "I apologize, I apologize."

Finally, he pulls her to his face. Serious. "I apologize, forgive me, Cheri." Then, "I don't care if you can see, or, not. You, understand. I'm going to kiss you, still." And, he does. The two of them warm into it, as Antoine's tenderness has saved the day. And, as , they build on this, long, awaited for moment. We await the night.

Chateux Suite

Immediately, from the car, they touch, and, kiss, hold, gripping with, swelling, embrace, as it transpires into ecstatic fever. Amidst his Châteaux, Antoine, and, Cheri, begin, fervorently, to undress. Themselves, and, each other.. Heated by their, new found, elation, they relate, and, tease, relate, and, tease, relate, and, tease. Curious, to the direction of this passion.

Voracious with this desire, and, overwhelmed, by the intense elation, they make it as far as the dining room table. Eagerly, he takes her in, settling her into his rapture. Caught within her wonder, they discover a new world. One, conducive to explore. Not, foreign, to affectionate terms. A world, in which they could, now, articulate the intimate. Liberate the exquisite.

Amid the fascination, she, is tenderly, wept. Truly, it had been some time, before, that she could lay claim to such purity. So, clear, were they about their new love, that they found themselves delivered onto ecstasy. Proceeding to express this fresh layer of bliss, again, and, again, and, again, and, again. Fade.

Enter Antoine's Châteaux, bedroom, morning, next day. Cheri sleeps in Antoine's bed. Half of her body lies beautiful, and, naked, outside the reach of the sheets.

Antoine sits at an easel, with a, mostly, painted portrait of our sleeping Cheri. He looks over at her. His eyes trail her body, as we see what he sees. Tracing, slowly, down, the length of her body, making the return trip to her visageal features, we discover her awake. Smiling, she eyes him, knowingly, as he has been caught.

Antoine, who has studied her most of the night, lay with her, enraptured, captivated by her amazing viability. This, unexpected, awakening, has breathed a new exuberance into his entire perception of life, of her.

Mesmerized, by her loveliness, and, blandishment, he thrilled to a start with epiphany. He would, expertly, capture that night, this morning with the genius of his artistry. He would paint.

Now, Antoine, didn't mind being disturbed, as his little angel was, now, alive, and, able to share in his joy. They, meet gaze, and, recognize each other once more. Cheri, who, now, notices him, painting, begins to rise. "What is that you're doing?" "No, no, no, don't move." He insists. She freezes. "What is it?"

"I am keeping my promise. I told you I could do better, and, I have. I'll show you, just stay." He instructs. "How long do I have to remain this way?" "Not long. I just need your basic landscape. I can complete the rest from memory."

Both of them drink in the silence, as, Antoine, busied himself with the replication of his muse, and, Cheri, poised, and, basking in the adoration, found herself answering Antoine's, game, of stealth, peaks of "do you remember" with flushed smile. "Good, I'm getting everything I need."

A moment, or, two more of quiet, and, Cheri, who's done a little observing of her own, decides to break the silence. "You don't seem like you're just from Paris." She probes. "That's because,

I'm not. I lived abroad, 'till I was eight." "ITinm..." She thinks. "What, exactly, moved you to Paris?" She proceeds further. "When the time is right, I will tell you." He confinns. "Right, now, I'm all to occupied with taking you in. Looking at you." He tumbles onto the bed, and, into a cozy embrace. "See?" "Oh, Antoine," she eases, "I only want to know to decide whether, or, not you are ever worth the distraction you have caused in my life." "A distraction I am, am I?" He quotes, inching toward her in playful threat. "A small one, but, nonetheless, yes." She reassuringly bubbles. Inching ever closer, he, without warning, lunges for her vulnerable frame, meeting her with kiss. They dangle in delicate balance, at the edge of the bed. He realizes what she cannot. Sight. She's lovely. Even, in all the ways which cannot be seen. In a swift moment, he realizes her journey, her unique life story. How she got all the way to Paris, to his arms. "Without sense of danger?" "Without barrier to freedom.?" Her Descartes puts him in a world, one in which he does not want to let her go. "Someone's precious package did become his prize." He thought. He wanted to care for her. Invest his being. Without the sacrifice of having to let her go. He wanted to keep her for his own.

Then, his life flashes before him. "With the life I lead, how do I make room for her?" He reviews. "Too hot. But, for now   His attention brings Cheri back into focus, and, again, he is with desire for her. As she has been amicable in her silent wait. He inhales this moment, and, in one breath manages to say, "Wow, you are beautiful."

Sight Unseen

Ah, in all of this romance, we still have Marcus.

Now, Cheri, unaware of her next door neighbor's trifles, breezes into the lobby of her safe gat away. So, it seemed. She ascends the elevator, exits, penthouse level, and, stops cold. "Hey." For, Marcus is camped outside her door. The familiar voice, triggers. Heart attack. She is dumbfounded, and, left without savvy words.

"I thought I'd find you here" He breaks the ice.

Cheri, is at odds as whether to be livid, or, warmhearted, at this unexpected appearance. For, she shed thousands of miles to flee from this uninspired affair. She suspended her feelings, to validate his own. Made play of his plans. Laid in wait of his wild overtures. Had enough. Ran worlds of revelation, to gain those of sweet freedom. What was she to do? What was she to do? What was she to do?

"Cheri," he starts. "Marcus...? What? How did you...why are you here?" She goes livid. What an interrupt. What an interference to the stride she's got going on in her life here. Just when she begins to live again, here comes the O.K. corral, policing events, once more. Unbelievable! "Hmm?" She thinks, attentive to his next line. "Well~.." He starts into the awkward silence. "You left before I had a chance to explain myself"

Cheri crosses to open her door. Determined to conquer this scenario.

"Marcus, per haps you left nothing said, because there was nothing for you to say." She starts in. "Matter of fact, I don't care why you cam;" she sighs with thought, "Marcus, I, really, don't want you here." She confesses.

Never before, had Cheri, at once, experienced such, natural, conflict. All at one, this score arrives on scene. Keen to the confrontation in await,

Cheri, preps, inmiediately, for the battle. The theme, obvious. He wants to hold on, she's committed to the release.

"Cheri, I came all this way. Let me say my peace."

Frustrated, yet, alert to the all, too real, factor of falling for old love, she files away all, distractions, determining to be objective only. Could she be tempted, once again? To return to Marcus' comfort zone, the abandon of self'? With all that she's discovered here, and, within? To become absolved, once more, into Marcus' dreams. Contracting, once again, to press her square peg into the compartmentalized life that is New York? No. Though there still remains a heart for Marcus, its hour has passed. And, though she still conveys the, residual, etchings of eight years, she's not going to buckle under the pressure of his latest rendition, playing wind to his plot. This is vowed. Instead, she will take heed, objectively, target main points, and, arrive, cleanly, at the best conclude.

"Come in She peels back the door, allowing him entrance.. .to talk.

Coles vs. Erickson

Exchanging casual pleasantries, en route to the common area, Marcus, and, Cheri, fmd a civil thread upon which to set about discourse. Cheri sets herself in position to hear him out. "Well, championship bout, Marcus. I'll yield court to you." She begins.

"Alright." Marcus commences. "Cheri, I'm going to start with an apology. For, all of the things," he sighs, "I thought were right." Cheri considers. "I know you to be a sensible woman. Sporting even. So, the only, natural conclusion is, if I were right, you wouldn't have run this far. Now, I can imagine your dilemma. Lone giri, new city. Knowing you, Cheri, you've started something that's going to test my nerve, and, fry my skill. With enough fmesse, I intend to reroute. Now, I know, right now, I'm not your favorite person. You don't like me very much. I don't, however, believe that eight years should go by without exacting the effort, and, affect it took to construct the relationship we worked to establish in the first place. We built a world, Cheri. And, based upon that, we've developed a bond. A code of honor. I'm not willing to permit its corrosion. I'm not willing to forfeit the battle, having the war mostly gained. I am not willing to walk away from my, vested, interests. Cheri, I want you to know that I came here with the intention, not of making complaint over minor misgivings, or, taking account of the injury. I came here with the specific purpose of having our broken ends mended. Of coming to a meeting of the minds. Of pushing through this nodulous way that we've made of this beautiful entity we have here. I don't want to give up. Pm not going to. I won't. Now, I've had my say. I want you to have your turn of expression." He gestures. 'Please."

Cheri, who, though, premature, has substantially, lived for this moment, takes pause, to approach. For, so long, he had, convened, guilty, and, stood, self-admittant to his wrong. For, once, he was right.

Redundantly, they had bouted., amidst quandary with this, or, that. Toiling, among, adroit, wear. Aiming, for the sky, constructed by moon. Missing, every, clear, note. She'd wondered, how, and, why, they'd, so often, they'd titan the clash, and, when, the clash, would tighten. They had more embattlements to relay, than memoir, affectionate. And, the, carole', why, t'was fading. The, allure was spent.

Though, touched, she knew that, now, was the, reckoning point. She must take up for herself. If, she did not, it could stand, testament, to her deservedness. Crossroads, afore, Cheri, now, was prime. Time had come, to seal her station. Loved, or, not, she was going to procure, for herself, only the positive. She could, secure, there. There, she could, feasibly, manage her own fate. For though, his words were kind, what he would do in public, would, surely, take place in the dark. She could afford to go forward, with ought New York, without Marcus; compromise.

This, sound, in mind, promotes maneuver. Cheri, takes position. Standing, she fmd her place, in prompt to Marcus. "I'll, begin, by clearing your mind of my opinion." She quells. "Contrary, to your, belief, I am, in no way, formed, nor, in light of your promulate. Counter-scored, I am, in no way, in dictate to your, breathend, appeal. Now, in relation to your, many, undressed, statements, I'll have to commend on the fly."

He squints in readiness for reply. "Marcus," she redirects, "I'll have you know that I can, only, be absolute, and, on the positive, when I tell you that, yes, I traveled this far, to move away from where we were going. Yes, in my growth, lam appreciate of your pursuit. Yes, thus, has begin something, altogether, appropriate in my behalf, that I wouldn't dream of curtailing, now. Though, I can't say that you haven't properly meted out with your, previous, regressions. Now, I want you to know, That, my love, our, love has come to terms that I must grant attention to. 'Where to go from here?' A question of the ages, don't you think?"

Marcus, for, once, is responsiveless. Never, in his life, could he forecast this weather in her. This, storm of an affection for her place amongst this, treasured life. Her language. It was so, formal, he hardly recognized her. Yes, she had grown. Yes, he was in the race for his life. Yes, he wanted her still.

"Now, that I've expressed it to you, thus, I'm going to say this." She sliced in again. "No, I'm not, in an overall sense, the least bit impressed by your, shrinking, attempt to quash, and, quell my advancement on this plain of existence. No, I am not the least bit afraid of a chance at this life without you. For, I am, fmally, at peace with who I am, and, who I want to be." Marcus, appears querulous, in disapproval, even. "Oh, come on, Marcus." She starts right in. "You've, neither, tempoed, nor have you ever been sport to my essence. To who I really am." He considers. "Sure, you've hinted, and, or, humored, as I suppose I must have you. However, I don't believe, anyway, that you've ever, really been, quite, on the money when it has come to, true, appreciation of me. You've puttered, stuttered, and, stumbled about it, but, you've never, quite, actually met me, even, halfway, to my, valid, truth. Which, leads to my third, and, final, 'no'. No, I'm neither, prepared, nor willing to return to that life of you, you, and, only you status. To play background, again. No!"

"How, can you refhse me this completely?" Marcus, fmally explodes. "Really, you come all the way out here, with me in pursuit of you, and, this is how you repay me? I'm insulted!" "You're insulted?" She blasts back. "Marcus, for years, now, you have performed, to the peak of your delight, mental, emotional, and gosh darned, if I don't have a father, just about, physical rape upon me. And, I will have it no more!" They are two bulls a twixt, upon recess.

"Okay, maybe I was wrong, Cheri, okay? In so many ways I probably was wrong. I know this. I also know that I've been acting out for a while, now. I won't make excuses for that. Yet are you going to let such a minute thing, in the, grand, scope of our lives just exhaust the existence out of eight years, just like, that?" He pleas with his might, his belly, and, his spirit, for all that it's worth.

"You know, it's, funny , you say that. Hnim. . . .minute? Yes, it's very interesting, because I didn't fmd it to be such a little thing." Marcus is on the verge of charging her, she continues. "As a matter of fact, I found it to be life changing. See, I've gotten a taste of that 'real world' you're always chastising me about. And, I like it! I'm not coming home."

"Cheri FIe contests. "what, Marcus? I'm sorry..." She intercedes. "You slipped and gave me an opportunity to really look at my life. One without you in it. I don't mind it!" She announces, while he fumbles for his trump. "look, next week I make parther. Off of that steam, Jacob, and, I are going to establish our own firm." He enthuses.

"Well, congratulations, sweets, and, candy, to you! Have some charm with you arrogance, why don't you." She, quips, inwardly, tarnished, taken with what she's about to relay.

"I'm not going to beg, Cheri." He relays. "That's not the only thing you won't be doing." She recovers, ready for anything that might be his next play. "Bulldozing me is not going to work, anymore, Marcus." Cheri, continues.

"You may have had me at 'Hello,' but, you lost me at green light. Be careful, because, somewhere, I just don't care to tow your line anymore.

"Give it some thought. Please. I mean, enjoy Paris, Hnim, but, do come home."

"No." Cheri, challenges, insists.

"I've hear 'no,' before. I didn't get to where lam by giving up. This isn't over, Cheri." "Well, then, for now, meeting adjourned." She conquers.

They dismiss within the formal style, appropriate to repass. Isolated, they recess in resign. Winded by the claim on battlement.

Cheri, withdraws, and, lays, momentary, claim to the, minor, victory. Holding tight to her dictation of stand, within the marked lines of her relative, declared freedom. Boundaries drawn, bivouac, in line, they shield their corners, in comparatives.

Cheri, in restitution to the evening's, hard fought, sentiments. Marcus, in script to his.

They redress, and, reshape the wounded forms of express, and, secure the points of advance in private cover.

Marcus, remitting to his place of defend. Cheri, resigning to hers.

Golden Advantage

They meet. Post, adventure, from, the hotel. At, The House of Momfort, Antoine's private palace. Where, he has already composed the, following, layer.

Cheri's, dispelled, yet, fortuitous happening, could not, and, did not hinder this, carefully, planned, long awaited, formulate, mapped out by Antoine. A man of many faces, he has, long, reserved this, rare, custom for someone, worthy. She, to a dictate, had proven the, reality, of his, fondest, wish. He had, but to, speak, into the air, and, there she would occur. Conceived.

Tonight, would be an, event, neither, one, of them, would, forget.

They pull up to a, brand, new, world of just, they two. She, can, sense, the state, though the descriptive has, not, yet, been offered.

A, fresh, awakening. The, vast, aire. The, robust, stimulant of, fragrance. The enchantment, of overture about the, lay. Prelude to conciliatory bliss, this, was, Antoine's, most, favorite, place, to be.

He, sees her out of the car, and, with preliminary introduction, he leads into his first, reveal. "This is where I come to be, me."

Cheri, soaks in the surroundings with, wonder. " I can sense it is breathtaking. Better than anything you have showed me, thusfar." "Indeed." He confirms. "You, bring me here, now, tonight, why?" She, carefully, inquires. "You know my ways, so far. I plan. I take risks. I plan." He begins. "I want, truly, to introduce, myself here." He asserts. "No more pretending. Come." Taking her by the hand, he scales the wallcway, and, escorts her, to the inside.

The swirl begins, as Cheri is completely taken within, the, colossal, allay of the place. The experience is outstanding, overwhelming, even. She, crispens, her breath at every intake, until, finally, she, "This feels enormous. What is it?"

Now, for some period of time, this matter of, confidence, was, exclusive, to those, qualified, for such, vested, and, inclusively, intended purposes. For, ages, this had been. The, choice, gentry of, solid, elect, poised, to, maintain, the, elite, standard, of, classification, entrusted, to this, class, of, titlemen. The,, day had been, full, with, treasured, discovery. Intrepid, motivations, and, audacious, reveal. Yet, tonight, would prove more, especially, sacred. To, the evening's extend, there would be, amazing, revelations, and, astounding, read-throughs. A meeting of the mind, that would satis~' him, completely. Seal the matter up, wholly.

"May, I direct you this way?" He begins.

He leads her to a, piqued, portrait, and, reads, "Here, 'Lord Antoine Thibodaux', present, and, commanding." A moment, and, then, the, register. "Why, Antoine, you're royal." She surprises. "That is my father." He affirms. "Yes, I am." He debonairs.

"Why this, is, marvelous!" She enthuses. "The man, and, his secret." she, intimates. "You, share this with me, so freely. Why, Antoine. And, why, tonight?" She delicates. "Listen, Cheri." He boars right in, "I know, you are no, dauntling, child. I, also, know, that you have become a, special, intrigue." He clarifies, immediately, then. "I know, it's so, very, early, yet, before you conduct your, skepticism," he tenders, "I'd like to tell you my story. Come, come with me."

We, follow, as he leads her, by the hand, from the, entryway ,into, the, sitting room.

Antoine, presents a bottle of champagne. We, layer, through episodes: of him, handing her a flute. Pouring, upon, wishes, refined. Speaking, to her, over sips, and, laughs. Finally, walking, her, into, Heritage Hall.

She is absolutely, overtaken, and, captivated by the, amassed, collection of, Family, busts, portraits, statues, and, vast mix, of other pieces, dear to the, legacy. There's a story, for, each, one, in his heart. His, hand, as, it, holds, hers. Teaching, her, his, form, of, sense. Presenting, her, with, as, yet, untouched, rose, before, the, garden, fountain. Sprinkling, the, peddles, as a rose, into, the, fountain, and, making, a wish.

Antoine, "So, how, is, it, that, you, see?"

"I have, a, sense, of, sight. It's, just, not, yours. I see, with, my, heart, and, sight, with, my, mind." She, insists. "Really. You, brave the world, in, your, solitary. T'is, a, strength, I, wish, to, admire." "I wish, I knew, more, of, it." He, assures. "In time, Cheri, you, will, come, to, know, that, I, do, take, the, pleasure, of, what, I, may, have, of, this, very, moment."

Walking, and, talking, she, fmally, takes, off, her, glasses. "You're, so beautiful." He confesses. Finally, they kiss. Antoine, dull-james, at, the, culdundrum. Then.

Enter: Momfort, Hall. Night, time. The, same. Antoine, begins, as, if, by, lullaby. " I, need, you to, hear, me, now. 'Once, upon, a, time He, begins. "Go, on. Through, to, the, ever-after, with, you." She, addends.

"Really, and, truly. Once, upon, a, time.. .there, was, a kingdom." He, begins. Kissing, her, thoughtfully, upon, her, brow.

"War, threatened, its, survival. Much, was, at, steak. And, the, king, had, serious, concerns." He, tenders. "Right. The welfare, of, the, people." She, adds. "Also, the, security, and, the, integrity, of, the, small, but, great, land. Alliances, were, made ...""And, these, partnerships?" As, Antoine, catches, on... "Yes, these, unions, of, state, were, established. And, great, promises, were, etched, in, stone. Indeed, a, future, brimming, with, guarantee." "And, the, spoils, of, the, country?" She, inquires. "Allotted, within, the, fashion, deserved." He, composes.

"How, do, 'you', work, into, this, story?" She, requites. "The, day, has, shown, you. Who, I, am, here." He, insists, carefully, placing, his, index, fmger, to, her, point, of, thought. "Now, I wish, you, to, see, my, soul." He, reclaims. Cheri, gathering, the, need, to, remain, silent, then, confesses... "Please, do, continue." She, elects.

"Through, a, series, of, fortunate, events. And, the, good, sense, that, comes, with, the, noble, instinct, of, natural, selection. I, became, a, Lord." He, insists. My, mother, was, a, duchess.

She, passed, along, not, long, after, I, was, born." He, continues. "I, miss, her, greatly." He, concludes.

There, is, a, pause. They, separately, engage, in, this, time. Only, to, meet, again, in, this, superior, moment. "Logically, then, your, father, must, be, a, duke." She, deduces. "True. My, sweet, little, wonder, you. Now, let's, play... 'Who, are, you?" He, positions, himself, to, listen. They, speak, and, touch, at, length.

Enter: Stratovarian. The, Red, Shoe. Day, same. We, see, Dana, waiting, in the, "hallway, of, chance." Ready, for, the, dance, of, her, life. She, is, called, forth. She, accepts.

Enter: Smits, Financial. Day, same. We, also, see, the, correlation, with, her, "big, presentation", at work. She's, really proving, herself.

Enter: House, of, Momfort. Momfort, Hall. Night, same. "I'm, one, of, two." Cheri, begins.

Enter: Stratovarian. The, Red, Shoe. We, see, Dana, introduce, herself. She, begins, dancing, with, her, assigned, partner. She, is, absolutely, beautiful.

Enter: House, of, Momfort. Momfort, Hall. Night, same. "You, have, a, brother, I, need, to, know?" He, offers.

Enter: Smits, Financial. Day, same. We , catch, Dana, as, she, wises, her, way, through, her, presentation. Witnessing, reactions, from, the, counsel... she, is, brilliant!

Enter: House, of, Momfort. Momfort, Hall. Night, same. "I'm, an, identical." She, identifies. "Astounding." He, replies. "Exactly." She, confirms. "And, your, family?" He, inquires. "I'm, New York, born. Manhattan, raised." She, confides.

Enter: Smith, Court, Hail. Day, same. We, take, note of, Richard Strathcrn, gracefully, litigating, his, case. Negotiates, the, trial, with, ease.

Enter: House, of, Momfort. Momfort, Hall. Night, same. "Heir, to, the, throne, of, Richard Strathern, the, first. Daughter, of, the, great, Mona Strathem.

Enter: Smith, Court, Hall. Day, same. We, witness, the, judge, rule, in, his, favor. We, montage, calls, to, his, daughters, over, a, triumphant, meeting, with, his, wife. Per, Cheri's, earlier, plea, and, Dana's, stereo, suggestion. "So, you're, first-born.?" He, furthers. "True. Only, my, sister..."

New York, City, Streets. Day, same. We, catch up, with, Dana, walking, 42~, Street. Victorious, after, having, sealed, the, deal. Guaranteeing, the, account. She, son, the, phone, celebrating, when, she's, nearly, sideswiped, by, an, on-coming, cab car. Verbally, accosting, the, car, Big Apple, style, she, continues, on. "Tough, seeing. Has, blinds, of, her, own."

Enter: House, of, Momfort. Momfort, Hall. Night, same. "How, God, saw, fit, to, have, you, here, with, me." He, relishes. "Who, of, your, surviving, family, do, you, correspond, with?" She, advances. Most. Then, you've, seen, my, local, familiars." He, enthuses. "1, suppose, as, long, as, you, have, position, you're, never, truly, alone." She, registers. 'Perhaps, one, day, we, may, further, the, import, of, these, binding, ties." He, imports. "For, now, come, close." He, gathers.

Driving, along, the, Paris, City, road, anight, under, the, blush, of, new, love, was, heavenly, as, Antoine, sang, of, theft, new, bind, amidst, the, night, sky. They, are, free!

A, call, comes, in, for, Cheri. T'is, Dana. Cheri, and, Antoine, drive, along, to, the, conversation. "I, understand, congratulations, are, in, order." She, genuines. "Yes! Thank, you. Mommy, and, Daddy, went, out, to, eat. We, celebrated, together. Wish, you, were, here. It's, unlike, you, to, miss, out. I, do, hope, it's, not, and, altogether, reality, for, you." She, statens. "I'm, supposed, to, interoperate, that...?" "Listen, I, know, you're, really, moved, out, about, the, whole, incident, with, Marcus, yet, I, must, contest, 8-years, is, 8-years, Cheri. You, began, there, you've, matured, there. He's, the, first, and, only, man, you've, ever, known. Don't, give, up, on, him, not, now, Cheri." Dana, pleas. "You're, really, going, to, ask, ask, me, to, cheat, myself, right, into, a, proverbial, saying, are, you? You, would, have, me, deny, myself, the, opportunity, to, fmd, real, movement, within, my, life? For, the, first, time, I'm, feeling, the, colors. Rather, than, just, the, black, and, white. Now, I'm, flying, where, before, I, was, only, pacing, the, ground. You, have, a, life, that, you're, satisfied, with, there. Well, I've, found, station, within, Paris. If, you, would, all, pardon, my, way, here." She, firms. "You, haven't, the, clearance, to, script, one, letter, Cheri?" She, places. A, moment, of, silence, then, "Probably, best, that, I, call, you, later." Cheri, insists.

"Cheri..." Dana, cuts, in. "Dana," Cheri, torts, "You're, A: into, my, business, as, usual. B:

beginning, to, demand, of, me, things, I, don't, want. I, don't, mind, the, suggestion, but, don't, force, Dana, don't, force. I, hate, your, strong, arm. I, hate, it." She, proves. "I, see. Yet, don't, you, think, it, best   Dana, adds. "Good-bye." Cheri, insists. "Oh, come, on..." Dana, intercedes. "Good-bye." Cheri, concludes.

She, clicks, off, and, proceeds, to, stare, out, into, the, distance. Antoine, who's heard, every, word, but, hasn't the, fill, of, innuendo, playfully, nudges, her. Both, smile, into, the, horizon. And, drive, on.

Introduction Upon Remuse

Enter: Paris, City, Street. Off, La Resistance, Alleyway. Night. They, two, steal, a, moment, against, the, night, air, achat.

"Now, that, I've, introduced. I'd, like, you, to, prelude, in, lou, for, me." He, contends. "What, really, brought, you, to, Paris?" He, extends. "With, all, good, intentions. The, rest, of, my, life." She, supplements. "You, intend, to, stay?" He, suggests. "Perhaps, I'll just, uproot, to, greener, pastures." She, quickens. "Well, with, such, a, pressing, agenda. How, long, will, you, in, truth, stay." He, commands. "As, long, as, I, need." She supplies. "How, long, until, you, travel, abroad, again?" She, permits. A, moment. Antoine, suddenly, is, called, back, into, his, reality. So, silent. Then, "Woa. Why, the, mystery?" She pulls. "Why, in, this, game, of, cards, one, must, be, prevailant and, attentive, to, the, meter." Cheri, concedes. "And, what, so, do, you, perceive, to, be, so, mysterious, about me?" He, convenes. "Curious." He, further, dares. "You, probe, to, inquire, of, my, heart. Yet, there, is, no, response, to, what, I, consider, a, simple, question." Cheri, confirms. "What, is, the, big, secret, Antoine?" Another, moment, of, silence. Awhence, he, looks, upon, her, with, inquisition. "Ah, yet. Mon, petite. I, cannot, tell, you, what, I, do." He, strongly, hints.

He, moves, to, embrace, her, by, the, forehead. She, draws, back. "Wait, just, your, minute. Why, not?" Cheri, insists. Not, a, moment, too, bright, nor, too, dark, and, Village, appears. In, the, nick, of, time, you, say? Yet, here, he, is, with, "You, may, not, have, to, tell, her, a, solitary, thing." He, finals.

Village, in, the, alleyway, with, a, few, other, members, refers, to, Cheri. "Perhaps, she, will, see, for, herself" Referring, back to Antoine, about, what, may, or, may, not, be, going, on. Village, simply, hints. "It's, on!"

Antoine, begins, to, protest. Village, interrupts, "There's, no, time. There, are, already, scouts, out, and, she's, marked." As, they, begin, to, double, back, to, their, underground, "She, and, yet, an, unexpected, casualty." As, Antoine, pauses. To, figure, out, who, that, could, be. Cheri, intercedes. "Antoine, what, is, going, on?" Cheri, demands. "I, will, tell, you, later." Antoine, insists. "No. I, need, you, to, tell, me, right, now." She, further, presses.

Antoine, immediately, grabs, for, Cheri. Abruptly, stopping, both, of, them, in, their, tracks. The, tone, now, deathly, serious. He, needs, full, cooperation, at, this, time. "There, is, no, time, to, tell, you, Cheri. Now, I, need, for, you, to, shut, up, and, follow, me."

He, measures, deeply, to, measure, the, success, of, his, translation. Cheri, nods, to, confirm, this, is, so. This, single, act, seals, their, fate. In, deeper, than, expected. He, gives, her, a, fmal, glare. This, immediately, understood, as, before. They, disappear, into, the, night. Sponsored, by, La Resistance

Sight on Flight

This, was, the, new, angle, he'd, periferrialled, into vision. Upon, introduction, never, had, he,. anticipated, the, alarm. Nor, the, quismed, company.

Into, the, dash, Antoine, hyper-connects, Villages, full, line, of, thought. At, hand, lies, Cheri's, safety, and, his, Coquette en plea. At, quantum, level, with, shear, flashings, of, the, eye, Antoine, instantly, charges, an, order, of, command. Reteeling, all, innocuous, ledgers. Finding, new, arrangement, in the, chain, of, care, Antoine, fmds, himself, locked, in , to, the, preme, design, of, location, Cheri, his, men.

Upon, inclusion, of, all, encompassing, stata, Antoine, relooves, lament, to, the, whole, of, the, edifice, sustained. Cheri, at, roads, extending, gratis, straits, to, the, tune, of, quinton frequency. Village, tight, grip upon, the, men, buzzes, with, steady, grace, upon, the, trail, of, direction, held, to, Antoine's, stead. The equipment, of; choice, hailed at the rampart, stages, flight, of, claim, to, Antoine's, journey, in, limbo.

The, impervious, cluster, makes, their, way, through, the, crowd, up, the, stairs, and, to, the, office. Twindswhile, just, beyond, reach, is, a, scout, escaping, notice.

Into, the, office, there is a, searing, anticipation. A, false, way, is, removed, and, floorboards, dilapidated, in, order, to reveal, the, works, of, art, for, transport. Artillery, and, further, endowments, are, steeply, prepared, upon, gather. Amidst, this, excitement: Robert, Antoine, and, Village, take conference.

"He's, upset, about the, heat, no, doubt." Reports, Village. Hinting, to, Antoine, Robert, refers, to, Village, as, well. "The, news, and, the, front, page, man."

Cheri, arisk, to, her, witness, feigns, the, breeze. Though, wheels, are, turning, and, the, pieces, coming, together, Antoine, takes, a, note, to, self. "Why, would, they, do, something, so, stupid? It, just, doesn't, make, sense." "Taking, out, your, brother, does, make, the, whole, thing, a, bit, more, complex." Village, laments. One, of; Antoine's, men, who, gather, and, load, the, artifacts, speaks. "Sir. We've, got, twenty, minutes." A, moment, and, all, especially, Antoine, connote, what, this, means. Harrah, is, short-lived, as, Antoine, seizes, the, opportune, to, smoothly, bark, out, commands, to, all, involved. Speaking, "Everyone, knows, their, position. Same, dance. Different, song. Let's, go. Move!" And, they, do. Spilling, into, the, false, opening, until, it, shuts. Closed.

Moving, along, the, interior, corridor, Cheri, is, reduced, in amuse. "Now, is, as, excellent, a, time, as, any, to, explain." She, controls. Antoine, moves, along, silent. Cheri, continues, her, extract. "The, surprises, have, been, lovely, but, this, is, heinous." Silence. Cheri, stops. "I'll, not, move, another, inch, until, I, Have, your, answer, somewhere." Village, scoots, along, just, ahead, of, them. "Au, merd! Here, we, go. Ca, mi, nervre!" He, exhausts.

Cheri, is, stopped. Adamant, about, her, position. Antoine, exhales, a, trail, back, to, pierce, her, sight. Both, understand this to be serious. An, executive, decision, must, be, made. He, will

have, to, extend, and, explain. Antoine, stops.

Village, who, does, not, believe, what, he, has, heard. The, action, taken, blazes, a, scope, of, disbelief, through, to, Antoine's, soul. Antoine, must, now, also, cover, for, this. Choosing, to, address, Village, and, maintain, control, of his, regime, Antoine, firmly, speaks. Once. Blocking, Village's, heat. "She, cannot, see." He, sharps. "She, is, blind." He, intrigues. "Interesting." Antoine, gives, a, look, of, dismissal. Village, moves, along. Antoine, returns, to, the, object, of, his, peak. "Move, with, me. I, will, tell, you." He, insists.

Along, the, way, many, things, flash, before, Antoine's, mind. The, reported, sightings. His, brother's, washed, body, upon, the, shore. The, timely, meeting, with, Cheri, shortly, there, before. His, uncle's, eariy, scout, and, warning, as, head, detective, of, the, Parisian, Police. As, this, extreme, routine, was, quickly, becoming, a, seeming, death, trap, with, its, members, being, picked, off, one, by, one, Antoine, had, much, to, think, through. Now, and, especially, with, Cheri, on, board, he, had, much, to, waver.

"I, deal, in, culture." He, confesses. "Its, preservation. Its, pronunciation." He, furthers. Our, establishment, is, one, of, 3, organized, smuggling, rings." He, offers. "In, partnership, to, the, world, of, the, black-market." He, concludes, through, the, fear, that, this, secret, will, repel, and, destroy, the, standing, built, thus, far. By, instinct, he, pulls, her, to. She, nearly, stumbles. "Antoine! Be, careful.." She, gasps, of, concern. "Always, know, your, right, out, of; folly. To, fashion, well, the, estranged. Keep, sharp, your, will, to, epicure, any, near, concern." Her, father's, words, ring, with, her, sense, of, anxiety, as, this, emergent, turn, her, life, is, taking, doesn't, at, all, sit, well, with, her. "I'm sony. We, need, to, move. Come, quickly." He pulls her back, into, his, stream, of, events. In, an, instant, Cheri, figured, she'd, go, as, far, as, her, courageous, little, heart, would, take, her. That, or, her, ego. Whichever, gave, out, first. "Just, guide, me. I, know, how, to, follow." She, starts.

As, they, hurriedly, make, march, down, throughout, the, interior, corridor, Cheri, is, full, of, questions. Making, **it,** her, business, to, detail, a, trail, of, notate, sealing, her, fate, in, joint, or, apart, from, Antoine. "A, need, for, black-market, art?" She, begins, insistent, upon a, gainsworthy, response. Required, in, the, midst, of; the, fresh, threat, to, her, life. "Government, control, and, sensoring." He, garnishes. "They, close, doors, we, open, others." "But, why? With all, you've, amassed, for, yourself. Why?" She, probes. "The, Government, and, its, red, tape. They, move, too, slowly, for, me. They, have, theft agenda. I, have, mine." "Yet, isn't, this, dangerous? I'm not, one, to invite, the, traverse, into, my, life." "Trust, me. It's, better, than, being, out, there, on, your, own. If, you, don't, mind, we've, got, to, move."

Instited, upon, magnitude, Antoine, accompanies, the, men, to, the, immediate, depart. To, the, wings, they, tear. Wristling, the, warn of; air, adjourned, to, time's, palate. The, great, escape, shall, not, miss, his, fmgers. Not, with, the, bellows, so, in cue. Antoine, and, his, men, load, on, and, into, the, awaiting, cavalcade. Cheri, the, surprise, doe.

Run Amiss

Inside, the, car, Antoine, continues, to, explain, while, the, others, run, the, drill. "Once, a, month, like, clockwork, we, deliver, the, goods. But, people, are, dying, now. Needless, to, say, the, game, is, changing, a, bit." With, that, Village, pulls, out, a, revolver. Cocks, gun. Cheri, is, in, arms. "Antoine... guns? Let, me, out." As, she, makes, attempt, for, the, door, Antoine, takes, hold, of; her, steadying, Cheri, for, clarification. "Cheri, these, are, all, too, necessary, encounters, for, this, leg, of; my, work." He, solves. "If, never, before, you're, going, to, have, to, trust, me, now. Do, you, understand?" "This, level, of, anticipate, makes, it, difficult. Do, you, understand?" Cheri, grates. "Believe, me, we've, survived, worse. You, can, do, this. You're, with, me. Now, come, on." He, coaches, securing, her, into, the, seat. Assuring, her, with, his, hand.

"This, is, where, it, gets, exciting." Village, proclaims." "Well, something, is, definitely, the, matter." He, warns. "So, be, alert." He, commands. "Don't, you, worry." Village, cues.

Speeding, along, into, the, night, Cheri, cannot, help, but, to, feel, solitary, and, at, odds. Having, just, leveled, at, "love, of; her, life", to, now, be, in , the, crutch, of; such, jeopardy. She, wonders, why the cards, won't, turn, a, lighter, shade. And, what, was, she, really, to, think, of; Antoine, now? A, privileged, fiend? A, cad, on, the, prowl? Had, he, so, completely, blinded, her, that, she, carted, all, abandon, to, the, stars? Clearly, she, had, better, sense. Clearly, she, vouched, for, a, life, that, worked. Well. Clearly, her, greater, mind, had, the, power, not, only, to, conceive, and, deduce, also, not, to, sit, by, and, allow, this, circumstance, to, get, the, better, over, her.

As, she, fidgets, in, thought, Antoine, steadies, her, with, the, touch, of, his, hand. Which, is, a, comfort, but, at, this, point, no, savior. The, car, ride, though, heightened, and, at, a, certain, serge, of; excitement, had, a, lonely, edge. As, Cheri, was, clearly, in, disappointment, at, Antoine's, past, time, harbors. And, Antoine, could, clearly, not, heroine, her, safe, elation, about, the, succeeding, prizewell. How, he, could, champion, back, the, adore, of; his, winsome, lady, would, be, the, theme, of; this, venture. For, he, must, win, this, night. Out, from, amongst, the, shadows, that, consumed, his, brother's, life. He, heartens, to, think, upon, hither, precious, cargo, in, his, stead, and, care. And, in, the, living, memory, of; Rembrandt, she, shall, go, untouched. Having, made, his, private, vows, he, barks, a, command. Confirms, others. And, they, march, off; into, the, night, at, the, order, of; business.

Operation: *Orient Express*

Await, in, the, night, it's, a, long, way, from, home. As, Jun, prepares, for, the, evening's, awaitings.

Arrival, upon, request, Jun, knows, this, delivery, to, be, remarked, dependable. In, house, poses. The, sea, breeze, cuts, fmely, into, his, intuition. Ancestral, paradigms, make, their, way, into, this, night. For, ages, have, staged, the, pace, of; time. Replete, with, remiss, this, hell-bliss, must, cut, short. For, the, report, of, fme-tunnage, is, bleefull, and, at, Stonehenge. Be, that, not, a, matter. Carrying, it, about. Big, dreams, aflight. To, honor, or, to, dishonor: that, was, the, question.

The, welcoming, party, is, in, position, as, our, group, pulls, up. They, engage, positions, for, the, routine, exchange. Antoine, heavy, on, his, heart. AS, this, means, more, to, him, than, what, they, know. For, his, brother's, shadow, prevails, upon, them. Upon, him. We, witness, the, two, groups, as, they, come, together.

Leader, of; the, pack, is, Jun Young. The, "law", or, connection, in, this, operation. All, settle, and, there, is, silence.

"There, seems, to, be, a, very, serious, problem, here." Jun, breaks, it, evenly. "My ,brother, is, dead. I, would, say, so." Antoine, gathers, and, promotes. "As, is, my, nephew. Which, brings, about, my, next, line, of, business." Jun, extravagates, as, one, of; Jun's, men, bring, out, a, captive, Marcus.

"Payback. Perhaps, we, can, engage, in, a, little, negotiation?" Jun, supplies. Marcus, bears, out, with, all, his, soul, at, the, sight, of; Cheri. "Cheri!" He, plunges. Antoine, shoots, Cheri, a, look, as, Jun, knocks, Marcus, cold, with, the, but, of; the, gun. Cheri, is, surprised, by, the, violence, and, caught, quite, off, guard, by, the, voice. Antoine, and, the, others, are, confused. "Marcus?" Cheri, inquisites. Antoine, whips, Cheri, into, his, arms. Aims, the, gun, at, Jun. "Who, is, this?" He, insists. "She, seems, to, know." Jun, cocking, the, gun, in, a, bit, of; fun, at, Marcus', head.

"Explain!" Antoine, demands. " I, don't, know, anything, but, that's, my, *fiancé!*" She, cries. "Fiancé?" Antoine, requests. "Well, not, any, more. I, called it, off. He, followed, me, here." She, testifies. They, had, to, have, gotten, to, him, through, me. Now, who's, watching, us, Antoine?" She, leads. Before, Antoine, can , respond, Jun, aims, the, barrel, at, Antoine's, temple. This, seizes, the, entire, group. Village, squints, in, amazement. All, men, take, aim. Jun, speaks. "I, don't, care, who, this, man, is. He's about, to, meet, my, nephew's, fate." Jun, cocks, the, gun, and, flexes, **it,** up, to, Marcus', chin.

Cheri, can't, handle, the, sheer, danger, she's, brought, Marcus', life, into. Breaking, away, from, Antoine, she, counts, her, steps, but, before, she, succeeds, Antoine, grabs, full, hold, of; he, again, cocking, his, gun, in, full, aim, of; Jun. "What, is, this, business?" He, cries, out, to, Jun, who, shoots, him, a, look, to, match, his, fierceness. "My, nephew, is, dead. What's, your, business?" He, cries, out, into, the, night. "who, is, this fiancé, of; yours, and, why, is, he, Jun's, prize?" Antoine, confides, to, Cheri. "Someone, I, left, back, in, New York." She, confesses. "I, don't, know, who, they, are, or, why, he's, here." She, affirms. "Him, being, here, is, my, fault. I've, got, to, do, something" She, demands. Antoine, instantly, calculates, plan. "You, run. When, I, say, jump, you, jump. When, I, say, land, you, land! Ready? Go!" She, begins, to, run, voraciously, awaits, the, call. "Now!" He, calls, out, with, all, his, might. "Now!" He, calls, out, again, for, her, land. Success! With, the, exception, of; Jun's, men, and, their, interception, of; her.

"Fine. You, can, take, his, place." The, exchange, is, quick. As, Jun, tosses, Marcus, over, to, Antoine's, men. Jun's, men, sweeping, up, a, startled, Cheri. Village, watches.

"No! Wait!" Antoine, cries, out, from, the, depth, of; his, soul. "I, will, do, no, such, thing." Jun, responds. "Negotiation, has, been, made!" He, demands. "No! They, are, innocent!, they, have, nothing, to, do, with, this." He, insists. "I, will go! Take, me!" He, pleas.

Jun, considers. Cocks, gun. "Alright. Let's, go." He, aSes. Another, quick, exchange, is, made. Cheri, is, thrown, to, and, caught, by, Antoine's, men. Antoine, is, lifted, onto, the, platform. "Antoine. What, now!" Cheri, calls, out. As she, is, frightened, and, cannot, see. As, Antoine, is, passed, off, into, the, hands, of; Jun, "That, will, be, all." He, declares. "I, don't, know, who, killed, your, brother. As, for, my, nephew... I'll, take, that, out, in, you." He, whispers, with, a, hiss, into, Antoine's, ear.

Jun, brings, out, the, crested, charm, that, used, to, wear, on, Village's, right, arm. We, hear, the, charmed, ring. See, it, glimmer, in, slow, motion. Antoine, studies, as, do, all, within, the, surround. "Left, for, me, is, the, "X", that, marks, the, spot. Cheri, is, invoked, into, a, flashback: We, see, what, Cheri, encountered, at, the, airport. Cheri: bumping, into, a, person. She, remembers, the, charmed, ring, of; the, bracelet. And, then, walking, on. As, she, gathers, herself We, see, the, back, of; Village. Walking, along, side, Jun Young's, nephew. The, last, time, he, was, seen. Cheri, caught, mid, revelation. Antoine, glares, at, Villages, right, arm. Eyes, in, full, recognition.

As, he, handles, the, crested, bracelet, t'winst, fmgertip. "You, can, imagine, my, surprise." He, gloats, and, mourns. Jun's, voice, catches, Antoine's, attention. IIe, spins, around, to, lock, eyes. Antoine, noticing, the, gun, ever, closer, to, his, useful, grip.

Cheri, held, by, Village, is, in, mid-revelation. Village, for, reasons, of; his, own, begins, to, reach, for, gun. He, cocks, it. Cheri, notices, this, and, tries, to, play, interference. Village, reacts. There, is, a, fight. The, gun, is, knocked, out, of, Villages, hands, and, into, the, water. Jun's, gun, is, then, exposed. In, position, for, Antoine's, grasp.

Village, sensing, his, trial, reaches, for, his, anide, gun. Antoine, with, very, little, struggle, knocks, Jun, out, of; the, way. With, gun, in, hand, he, spins, around, to, shoot.

Village, with, gun, in, hand, rises, to, shoot. The, shot, fired, from, Antoine, hits, Village, right, between, the, eyes. Shot, fired, form, Village, grazes, Antoine's, head.

Cheri, on, the, ground, with, Villages, lifeless, body, hears, Antoine's, complaint. Takes, it, for, the, same, fatal, blow. "No!" She, cries, out.

Everyone, the, whole, place, falls, silent. Antoine, snaps, his, eye, open. "Cheri?" He, calls, out, respectively. "Antoine!" Cheri, remits, thankfUlly.

Jun's, men, help, him, up, as, the, sound, of; sirens, approach.

Jun, to, his, men: "We, leave, now!" Antoine, to, his, men: "Do, as, prepared. And, Let's go!"

Antoine, and, Cheri, feel, their, way, as, Antoine, trots, from, the, dock. "Antoine!" "Cheri!" Then, "Cheri!" A voice, calls, out It's, Marcus. Cheri, stops, cold. Turns, around, to, Marcus, who, is, still, bound. "Will, you, help, me, out, here? By, the, way, Let's, go, ourselves." He, exclaims, and, demands.

Cheri, whips, around, to, Antoine. "Do, I, have, your, heart?" Antoine, doesn't, like, the, timing. "Must, we, go, through, this, right, now?" "Come, on, Antoine." She, urges. "I'm, scot-free. I, won't, budge." She, insists. "If; I, don't, have, your, heart, I, sure, as, Adam, won't, volunteer, for, this."

Police, begin, to ,pull, up. One, of; Jun's, men, gives, the, command, in, Chinese. Given, the, obvious, circumstances, they, must, move.

"So, what's, it, going, to, be?" Cheri, is, hot, with, insistence. For, there, is, a, nerve, of; anxiety, that, she's, got, to, pull.

Antoine. Frozen. Inches, toward, the, boat. The, silence, makes, this, instant, the, answer. Cheri, whips, around, to, Marcus. "Cheri!" He, relieves. Before, she, is, able, to, approach, a, gear, shift, in, the, boat, snaps, Antoine, into, reality, causing, him, to, cry, out, to, the, first, thing, on, his, mind. "Cheri !" Not, up, for, games. Cheri, calls, out, in, demand, and, disgust. "An, answer!" The, men, on, board, grow, anxious. Roger, calls, out, "This, is, tight. We, must, go." Antoine, knows, this, this, the, hour, of; reckoning. Giving, attention, to, his, heart. **He,** exclaims, "Yes!"

That's, all, she, needed, to, hear. She, takes, a, moment, to, look, back, at, Marcus. Antoine, campaigns, for, her, speed. "Yes. Cheri, the, answer, is, yes! Come!"

She, Looks, over, to, Marcus. The, time, left, is, reduced. They, call, out, to, each, other. She, goes, to, him. He, is, not, far, from, her. She, assists, in, ,freeing, him, of his, bindings, but, leaves, one, cuff, to, the, rail. Marcus, is, aghast. "What, are, you, doing" Wh. . . what, is, this" Quickly, she, crouches, down, to, his, level. Upon, explain: "This, is, for, the, eight, years. For, making, me, feel, like, I, wasn't, worth, it."

More, police, arrive. They, begin, round, up, formation. Antoine's, men, begin, to, take, off. Robert, calls, out. "Antoine!." Antoine, protests, "I, know, we, must, go." Antoine, leaps, on, board. Cheri, sensing, this, laps, around. Abandoning, Marcus. "Wait!" She, cries, out.

She, counts, her, steps. Sprinting, for, the, boat. Antoine ,is, intense, with , will, for, her, to, make, **it,** upon, the, boat. She, continues, to, race, to, the, dock, and, stops.

Police, are, moving, in, on, Marcus, who, watches, helplessly. They, begin, to, pursue, Cheri. Antoine, yells, for, assistance. "Help, me!" Roger, joins, chorus. "Hey! Right, here!" Jun, who, is, near, enough, by, to, notice. Takes, hint,. Barking, out, command. "Prepare, to, break!" Then, to, Antoine, "Tell, her, to, jump, at, my, command!" Antoine, takes, the, sign, and, relays, the, message, to, Cheri. "Cheri. You're going, to, have, to ,trust, me. Jump, when, I, tell, you."

They, circle, back, around. Jun, commences, with, the, distraction. In, hot, pursuit, the, Police, call, out, over, dispatch, "Close, out, the, Harbor! I, repeat. Close, out, the, Harbor. We, need, back up!" Jun, in, place, calls, out, to, Antoine, "Now! Right, now!" Antoine, in, turn, cries, out, to, Cheri, "Now! Cheri, now!" Cheri, races, the, boat, races. Both, on, delicate, timing.

Police, are, in, the, distance, launching, counter, attack. The, Captain, breaks, hold.

Cheri, fierce, with, focus, dashes, for, the, boat, leaping, into, the, air. The, boat, slowing, just, enough, for, her, to ,be, caught, by, Antoine, mid-air. Who, rolls, with, and, shields, her, upon, landing. Seeing, the, success, Jun, announces, the, command, to, "Go!"

High-speed, to, the, bridge. The, police, give, chase. Firing, shots, at, Jun, Antoine, and, their, men. They, return, no, fire. Their, race, is, closing, for, the, bridge. One, of; the, shots, hits, Roger, in, the, shoulder. "Man, down! Roger's, down!" One, of; the, crew, call, out. The, boat, careens, into, Jun's. They, loose, momentum. Another, crew, member, takes, control.

Jun, has, to, make, the, executive, decision, to, shoot IIe, does. Right, into, the, gas, tank.

The, explosion, throws, off; all, boarding, officers. This, buys, the, some, time. However, the, blow, knocks, Cheri, into, the, water. "Merd!" Antoine, cries, out.

By, this, time, Jun' s, boat, is, beyond, the, Harbor, and, scot-free. Antoine's boat, must double, back, for, Cheri. Jun, knows, that, he, must, cover. As, the, police, begin, to, fire. Antoine's, men, begin, to, maneuver, and, Antoine, successfully, retrieves, Cheri, from, the, water.

"Circle, back. So, that, I, can, get, a, shot." Jun, commands, his, men.

They, do. As, Antoine, pulls, her, on, board, another, of; his, men, is, shot. "You're, expensive." Antoine, courts, in, the, heat, of; fire. Cheri, breathless, and, thankful. Replies, "To, happily, ever, after. Please."

Antoine, and, his, men. As, well, as, Jun, and, his, men, begin, to, return, fire. Antoine, too, aims, for, the, gas, tank. There, police, boat, #2, explodes.

Antoine, and, Jun, speed, off, past, the, harbor. Calling, out, to, each, other, the, regress: "By, the, way. Do, you, have, my, business?" Jun, negotiates. "As, always." Antoine, sports. As, he, snaps, his, remaining, men, into, this, series, of; exchange. As, Antoine's, men, pass, over, several, cases, of; goods, Jun's, men, return, with, two, cases, of; cash. All at, high, speed.

They, interchange, with, smile. "I, go, my, way. You, go, yours." Jun, offers. "Thank, you." Antoine, confers.

Sirens, glare, as, they, speed, off, **into, the, night.** Antoine, holds, dear, to, Cheri. As, Antoine's, men, conclude, the, patching, up, of; Roger, and, the, other, suited, body, member.

Rag Time-Run

After, a, time, amidst, the, water. Antoine, and, Cheri, took, note, to, traverse, time, upon, dry-land. After, all, Coles, beat, Erickson. The, speed, chase, beat, that. And, the, race, for, the, Harbor, took, all. Now, was, a, time, for, rest, and, fortitude.

On, train, en, scenic, route, we, catch, up, upon, Antoine, and, Cheri. In, recline.

"Our, slow, boat, to, china?" Cheri, restfully, inclines. "Or, perhaps, it's, time, that, I, retire, and, we, make, a, family." Antoine, seriousens. "International, espionage, or, the, house?" She, wits. "Mmm. Tough, decision." She, uptakes. "You?" He, sharpens. "Becoming, one, of, us?" He, brightens. "Let's, go, for, the, house. Shall, we?" They, smile, in, kind. And, chortle, a, bit. "Not, bad, back, there. If; I, do, say, so." She, adds. Antoine, raises, a, toast, "Here, to, new, beginnings." He, begins. "And, to, you. My, sweet, muse." He, continues.

On, the, toast. We, hear, the, charmed, ring, of; the, crested, bracelet.

"I, like, that." She, corresponds. "I, know. You, do." he, heroines.

At, that. They, were, off, to, their, happily, ever, after."

THE END